Praise for Skull and Pestle: New Tales of Baba Yaga

"In stories of greed, revenge, longing, and resolve, the authors address themes of female bonding, the relationships between mothers and daughters, and the value of mentors passing on knowledge to students...Readers will find this an enchanting set of takes on a legendary figure."

—Publishers Weekly

"These are women's stories in that they're about the bargains women make and the cost of the knowledge and salvation that women buy for themselves as they make their way through the world. Although Baba Yaga functions as a mentor, her guidance is brutally realistic: You'll be asked to do the impossible in order to survive, and there will always be a cost."

—Foreword Reviews

Skull & Pestle: New Tales of Baba Yaga

❧ ⸙ ❧

Anthology Edited By

KATE WOLFORD

World Weaver Press

Published by World Weaver Press, LLC
Albuquerque, NM
www.WorldWeaverPress.com

Cover illustration © 2018 by Russell Thornton
Cover layout and design by Sarena Ulibarri

*

First edition: January 2019
ISBN-13: 978-1732254626
ISBN-10: 1-7322546-2-1

Also available as an ebook

SKULL AND PESTLE: NEW TALES OF BABA YAGA

TABLE OF CONTENTS

INTRODUCTION
Amanda Bergloff

A wild wind begins to blow. Leaves swirl in the air, and the trees of the forest groan and shake. Then, something appears overhead. A giant mortar (a bowl for grinding food) flies through the air with a nightmarish occupant. The frightening features of the witch are all the more pronounced when she bares her sharp iron teeth which gleam in the moonlight. Perched in the mortar, skeletal knees up to her chin, she uses a pestle held in her right hand as a rudder to move across the treetops quickly, while her left hand sweeps her wake with a silver birch broom. The accompanying shrieks that follow her die down after she passes, and the forest is once again, still…

And an enigmatic figure from Eastern European folklore enters our modern consciousness with this book, and its collection of tales, in the form of the intriguing Baba Yaga.

Baba Yaga, the mysterious, fearsome witch with the penchant for either helping or eating people, is a well known character in Slavic mythology. Her name, Baba means "old woman" or "grandmother," while Yaga means "witch" or "wicked," and in the different folkloric versions of her, many things remain the same as to how she's portrayed.

This supernatural crone is usually described as being very old and skinny even though she has the appetite of many men. Her long nose touches the ceiling when she sleeps on top of a large oven, the same one she uses to cook anyone who shows up to her hut and fails to perform the special tasks she gives them. She is also known for her iron teeth, which presumably help her in eating people who don't meet her expectations.

Baba Yaga gets around the forest, either on the ground or in the air, by sitting in a large mortar and using a pestle to guide her, while sweeping away her tracks with a silver birch broom.

Stories about her mainly take place at her wooden hut, located deep in the Russian forest and usually involve girls or women who come to her for help or advice. This is tricky for the innocent heroine, as Baba Yaga's hut has a fence of human bones topped with skulls with glowing eyes that warn the witch of intruders. However, once past the fence, the hut itself is difficult to enter, as it stands on giant chicken legs and is constantly spinning around until the correct words are said that allow one to stop it from moving and enter.

The most well-known tale Baba Yaga appears in, "Vasilisa the Beautiful" (from *Russian Fairy Tales*, collected by Alexander Afanasyev between 1855 and 1863), tells the story of the beautiful and kind Vasilisa. Living with her wicked stepmother and jealous stepsisters, Vasilisa is sent by them to Baba Yaga's hut with the hope that the witch will eat her, but instead, the witch gives Vasilisa seemingly impossible tasks to do. When Vasilisa proves her worth to Baba Yaga, the witch sends her back to her family with something that ends up destroying them, thus freeing Vasilisa from her evil stepmother and stepsisters. So, Baba Yaga goes between frightening witch-villain to maternal savior all within the same story.

This paradox in her behavior is seen in many tales and makes her unique among figures in folklore. While witches in European traditions behave predictably by taking on the role of villain to harm the protagonist, Baba Yaga's mercurial character has her also aiding the ones she finds worthy after they pass the grueling and impossible tasks she gives them. Despite her apparent cruelty at first, she is always shown to honor any bargain she has made, whether she is pleased with the outcome or not. The heroine of the story usually walks away better off after her interactions with Baba Yaga and with something that will defeat those who must be defeated in the course of the tale. Baba Yaga's complex and contradictory nature reflects a realistic aspect of the world, in all its positive and negative forces, through questions and answers, knowledge and ignorance, life and death.

Yet, Baba Yaga ultimately calls to the outsider in all of us. Living on her own terms, outside of society's conventions and expectations of behavior or standards of beauty, she embodies the wildness of nature, and her power stems from her refusal to be tamed. She is an inspiring and complicated Earth Mother, an eternal spirit that stands outside of time.

In *Skull and Pestle: New Tales of Baba Yaga*, anthologist Kate Wolford has collected seven unique tales of this iconic witch that will transport you from a Tsardom far away beyond high white mountains and vast icy steppes, to a swamp in Alabama, to impossible paths lit by the supernatural eyes of a skull, and beyond.

In "Vasilisa the Wise," Kate Forsyth tells the classic Russian fairy tale of a girl with a pure heart who encounters Baba Yaga and performs the impossible. Lissa Sloan's "A Tale Soon Told" is a bittersweet reflection on a life seen in three different phases under the subtle guidance of the all-knowing grandmother. "Baba Yaga: Her Story" is author Jill Marie Ross' take on Baba Yaga's origins, of Koschei the Deathless and how lost souls can find one another and become family.

Set in a place where folktales and the horrors of World War II tragically meet, "The Partisan and the Witch" by Charlotte Honigman tells the tale of a girl's bargain with Baba Yaga for weapons to kill three who cannot be killed. Here, the dead can help the living, and a blessing can scare even a powerful witch.

A mysterious old crone in the swamplands of the American South helps a motherless girl find her true calling in Szmeralda Shanel's "The Swamp Hag's Apprentice." In "Boy Meets Witch" by Rebecca A. Coates, doing impossible chores for a witch is the least of a boy's problems once the spell he asked her for takes effect.

And the anthology culminates with Jessamy Corob Cook's "Teeth," a tale of sisters, jealousy, guilt, sacrifice, and revenge.

So tell the hut to stop spinning so you can pour yourself a cup of tea from the samovar. Sit by the warm fire to enjoy these stories, and when you're done, think of the favor or question you would like to ask, because Baba Yaga is waiting…

Baba Yaga knows all.

***

Amanda Bergloff is an editor and author who writes modern fairy tales and speculative fiction. Her work has appeared in various anthologies, including *Stories from the World of Tomorrow, Frozen Fairy Tales, After the Happily Ever After,* and *Uncommon Pet Tales.* She is also editor-in-chief of *Enchanted Conversation: Fairy Tales, Folktales, and Myths* at fairytalemagazine.com.

VASILISA THE WISE
Kate Forsyth

Long, long ago, in a Tsardom far away beyond high white mountains and vast icy steppes, there lived a merchant and his wife. They had only one child, a daughter named Vasilisa, and the three of them lived together in great peace and contentment. One day the merchant's wife fell ill. She called her daughter to her, and gave her a tiny wooden doll.

"My dearest child, I am dying." With difficulty, she sat up and pulled out a tiny wooden doll that she pressed into Vasilisa's hands. "With my blessing, I leave to you this doll, which my mother once left to me. Carry it with you always and never show it to anyone. When evil threatens you or sorrow befalls you, take it from your pocket and give it something to eat and drink. You may then tell it your trouble, and it will help you." She kissed her little daughter on the forehead. Shortly afterwards, she died.

Vasilisa grieved greatly for her mother. Her sorrow was so deep that when night came, she lay in her bed and wept and did not sleep. Eventually she remembered the wooden doll. She rose and went to the kitchen, where she tore off a fragment of bread and poured out a thimbleful of milk and set it before the doll.

"I am so sad, little doll. Can you help me?" she whispered.

The doll's eyes began to shine like fireflies, and suddenly it became alive. It ate a morsel of the bread and took a sip of the milk, while Vasilisa told her all her woes.

"Do not sorrow and do not weep, but close your eyes and go to sleep. For morning is wiser than evening," the little doll said.

So Vasilisa lay down, the doll in her arms, and the next day her tears were less bitter. So it went on for a long time, with the doll comforting Vasilisa and giving her the strength to go on.

The merchant grieved for many months too, but the time came when he thought it best to marry again. His eye fell on a widow with two daughters of her own. They would be company for his little Vasilisa, he thought, and so he married the widow and brought her home as his wife.

Now Vasilisa's step-mother was a cold, cruel woman, who had married the merchant for the sake of his wealth. She had no love for Vasilisa. All day she screeched about the house: "Come, Vasilisa! Where are you, Vasilisa? Fetch the wood, don't be slow! Start a fire, mix the dough! Wash the plates, milk the cow! Scrub the floor, hurry now!"

Her own daughters lolled about, curling their hair and painting their toenails, while Vasilisa's fingers were worked to the bone. She had the help and comfort of her mother's little wooden doll, however, and so she was able to endure. Each night, when everyone else was sound asleep, she would creep from her bed and find scraps of food for the doll.

"I am so lonely, little doll. Will you talk to me?" she would say.

The doll's eyes would shine like glow-worms. It would comfort her and tell her stories of the past. And while Vasilisa slept, the doll would prepare all the work for the next day, so Vasilisa did not have to toil so hard.

One day the merchant had to travel to a distant Tsardom. He bade farewell to his wife and her two daughters, and kissed Vasilisa goodbye. She watched him ride away with an awful sinking in her stomach, fearing what her step-mother would do.

That night the merchant's wife called the three girls to her and gave them each a task. Then she went about the house, secretly dousing every fire and candle till it was so dark the girls could not see.

"It is now too dark to work," the step-mother said. "One of you must go to Baba-Yaga's house to ask for a light."

Vasilisa shrank back. Baba-Yaga was a witch who gobbled up people the way wolves devoured rabbits.

"I'm not going," said the eldest daughter. "I am making lace, and my needle is bright enough for me to see by."

"I'm not going," said the second daughter. "I am knitting stockings, and my needles are bright enough for me to see by."

But Vasilisa was spinning flax, and she could not see a thing.

Her step-mother laughed and said: "Vasilisa must go! Get yourself to Baba-Yaga's house this minute, Vasilisa, and ask her for a light." And she pushed Vasilisa out the door and locked it behind her.

Vasilisa shivered with fear. The blackness of night was about her, and the rustling and murmuring of the forest, and the wild cold wind. She took out her little doll, and drew a crust of bread from her pocket to feed it.

"O dear little doll, I must go to Baba-Yaga for a light, but I'm afraid she'll eat me with one great bite. Whatever shall I do?"

The doll's eyes began to shine like two stars and it became alive. It ate the crumbs and said: "Do not fear, Vasilisa, my dear. No harm shall come while I am here."

The light from the doll's eyes beamed out through the darkness, revealing a narrow, crooked, winding path through the forest. Holding the doll close, Vasilisa started out on her journey.

The forest was tangled with thorns and hung with grey moss. Vasilisa stumbled along the path, following the light from the doll's eyes. When she heard hooves galloping behind her, she leapt out of the way. A man crouched on the back of a horse raced past. He was arrayed in white, and his horse was white as milk, and the harness was silver. As he passed by, the darkness lifted and birds began to sing. Vasilisa's steps quickened.

For long hours she hurried along, and then another horse galloped past. The rider was robed in red, and his horse was red as blood, and the harness was scarlet. As he passed her, the sun rose high into the sky.

Vasilisa was hungry and tired and footsore, but she pressed on, following the path deep into the forest. The shadows lengthened, and the sky dimmed. Then a third man on horseback came galloping up. He was clad in black, and his horse was black as coals, and the harness was made of iron. As he passed her, the sun set and the forest was plunged into darkness. Vasilisa clutched her doll closer, and kept on following the narrow path.

A long time later, she saw a light ahead of her. In a clearing amongst the trees, a wretched hut stood on skinny chicken legs, surrounded by a fence made of bones and crowned with skulls. All the eyes of the skulls were lit up and were gleaming red.

The house began to dance about on its chicken legs, jumping up and down as if in anticipation. The trees groaned, the branches creaked, and the wind howled. Dry leaves whirled up and spun around Vasilisa, who shrank back in fear.

A huge iron mortar skidded along the path. In it was crouched an old woman, her arms and legs as thin as toothpicks, her filthy grey hair whipping behind her. In one hand she held a pestle, which she used to propel the iron tub forward. In her other hand was a kitchen broom made of silver birch twigs, which she used to sweep away her tracks. Her teeth were iron, sharpened to points.

Sniffing all around her, Baba-Yaga cried: "I smell flesh and blood so sweet, who is here for me to eat?"

Tucking her doll safely away, Vasilisa stepped forward. Her knees were trembling. "It is only me, Vasilisa. My stepmother sent me to you to borrow some fire."

"Did she? How very kind of her," the old witch said. "Well, I give nothing away for free. You must work hard to earn your fee. If you fail, I'll guzzle you for tea." Then Baba-Yaga cried: "Unlock, my bolts so strong! Open up, my gate so wide!"

The gate of bones swung open, shrieking as if the motion caused it pain. Baba-Yaga flew in.

Vasilisa crept behind her, but a birch tree by the gate lashed Vasilisa with its frail, dry branches.

"Do not whip the maid, birch tree, it was I who brought her here," said Baba-Yaga.

A thin, mangy dog snapped at Vasilisa.

"Do not bite the maid, dog, it was I who brought her here," the witch said.

Then a bony cat lashed out at Vasilisa with its sharp claws.

"Do not scratch the maid, cat, it was I who brought her here."

Baba-Yaga smiled at Vasilisa, showing her pointed iron teeth. "You see, you will not be able to escape easily from here, Vasilisa. My cat will scratch you, my dog will bite you, my birch tree will lash you, and my gate will bar your way."

Vasilisa tried hard not to show her fear, putting her hand inside her pocket to touch the little wooden doll. *At least I am not alone,* she told herself.

All the while, the witch's hut kept spinning around on its skinny chicken legs, shrieking and creaking.

Baba-Yaga struck the ground with her pestle and cried, "Hut, hut, turn your back to the forest and your front to me."

Slowly the hut stopped spinning, and came to rest facing them. Its door screeched open, and a rickety ladder slid out. The witch flew in, but Vasilisa struggled up the ladder. It was much bigger inside than seemed possible from the small size of the hut. A huge black stove with a red fiery mouth dominated one wall, while dozens of legs of ham and plucked birds hung with ropes of onions and garlic from hooks in the ceiling.

"I'm hungry," Baba-Yaga said. "Feed me well, or I shall decide to eat you instead."

So Vasilisa hurried to find the old witch something to eat. She brought her a pot of beetroot soup and a loaf of bread, but Baba-Yaga was still hungry. She brought her a haunch of ham and fried up six dozen eggs, but Baba-Yaga was still not satisfied. So Vasilisa cooked up twenty chickens, forty geese and sixty doves, which the old witch devoured in just a few bites.

"I'm thirsty," Baba-Yaga shrieked. Vasilisa brought her beer by the barrel and milk by the pail. Soon nothing was left but a heel of dark bread and a dribble of milk. Vasilisa ate and drank eagerly, but made sure to keep a little back for her doll.

Baba-Yaga glared at her with bloodshot eyes.

"Now, Vasilisa," said she, "while I have my nap, you must take this sack of millet and pick it over seed by seed. And mind that you take out all the bad ones, for if you don't, I shall eat you up."

And Baba-Yaga stretched out on her enormous iron stove, closed her eyes and began to snore. When she was sure the witch was asleep, Vasilisa took the thin crust of bread, and the few drops of milk, and offered it to her doll.

"I am so afraid, little doll. The task she has set me is impossible. Can you help me?"

The eyes of the doll began to shine like two candles. "Do not sorrow and do not weep, but close your eyes and go to sleep. For morning is wiser than evening."

Vasilisa did not think she could possibly sleep, but she was exhausted from her long journey. She curled up on the floor, shut her eyes and soon her breathing relaxed.

The doll called out:

"Birds of the air, hear me,
There is work to do, you see.
Come in answer to my call,
You are needed, one and all."

Flocks and flocks of birds came flying, more than eye could see or tongue could tell. They began to sort the seeds, the good into one sack and the bad into another. And before they knew it the night was gone and all the work done.

When Vasilisa awoke and saw the sacks of sorted seeds, she thanked the birds and promised to never forget to put out food for them, then hugged her doll tightly.

"Beware, Vasilisa, keep your wits alive, if this day you are to survive." And the little wooden doll crept wearily into Vasilisa's pocket again.

When Baba-Yaga woke, she was amazed and angry to find the task had been done. Scowling and growling and stamping about, she told Vasilisa to scrub the house from top to bottom, and milk the cows, and peel a great pile of muddy potatoes. "I'm off to hunt. Mind, now, if you do not do it all, I shall eat you up."

Vasilisa nodded and watched as the witch jumped into her iron mortar. Just then, the man in red galloped out on his blood-red horse, and the sun rose high into the sky.

"Who are the horsemen?" Vasilia dared to ask, remembering them from the forest.

Baba-Yaga grinned, showing her iron teeth. "They are my Bright Dawn, my Red Sun and my Black Midnight."

"Where do they ride?" Vasilisa asked.

"They hunt each other across the sky."

"But why?"

Baba-Yaga looked at Vasilisa, and her grin grew wider and wider, so that her iron teeth glittered.

"Never mind," Vasilisa said, holding up both hands and backing away.

Baba-Yaga laughed. "She is wise for one so young. And now I hunt!" She brought down her pestle, and with a spray of sparks the mortar launched into the sky, the old witch hunched inside, sweeping away her tracks.

Vasilisa fed the cat and the dog, whose bones showed sharp under their skins, and watered the birch tree's parched roots. Then she fed her little doll and begged it for help. And the doll called out in ringing tones:

"Come to me, mice of house and field,
there are pots to scrub and potatoes to peel!
Come in answer to my call,
You are needed, one and all."

And the mice came running, swarms and swarms of them, more than eye could see or tongue could tell, and before the day was over the work was all done.

Night fell as the black horseman galloped past the gate. The eyes of the skulls crowning the fence glowed red. The trees groaned and the wind howled, and Baba-Yaga came riding home, sweeping behind her with a broom.

She was furious when she saw how everything gleamed, and the great pile of clean, white vegetables. She stamped about and mumbled and grumbled, and after she had eaten an even bigger dinner than the night before, she went to bed.

The third day passed in much the same way as the first, though this time it was the ants that came to Vasilisa's help. Baba-Yaga was angrier than ever, and when she went to bed Vasilisa heard her mutter:

"Crack her bones and suck them dry,
Roast her flesh and boil her eyes,
Mash her brains and make mince-pies,
Tomorrow that girl shall surely die!"

Once again Vasilisa put some milk and bread before her doll, and watched it come to life, its eyes glowing like tiny suns.

"You must escape," the doll told her.

"But how? Will the cat not scratch me, the dog bite me, the birch tree whip me, and the gate bar my way?"

"Think what you may do for the cat and the dog and the tree and the gate, then they will think what they can do for you."

Vasilisa thought hard. Then she hugged her doll and put it into her pocket, and crept through the house, finding what she needed. She gave the cat a bowl of cream, and the dog a thick slice of red beef. She watered the birch and cleared away the weeds choking its roots. Then she took some oil and greased the hinges of the gate of bone. The gate swung open for her, and she ran through. Only the red glowing eyes of the skulls saw her pass.

Seeing them, Vasilisa thought, "I can't go home without any fire or my stepmother will be angry." So she lifted down one of the skulls and used it to light her way through the forest. By the time the white horseman galloped past she was far away.

Baba-Yaga woke and, seeing that Vasilisa was gone, bounded to her feet.

"Did you scratch Vasilisa as she ran past?" she asked the cat.

"No, I let her pass, for she gave me a bowl of cream," the cat replied. "I served you for many years, Baba-Yaga, but you never gave me so much as a drop."

Baba-Yaga rushed into the yard. "Did you bite Vasilisa as she ran past?" she asked the dog.

"No, I let her pass, for she gave me meat to eat. I served you for many years, Baba-Yaga, but you never gave me so much as a bone."

"Birch tree, birch tree!" Baba-Yaga roared. "Did you whip Vasilisa?"

"No, I let her pass, for she watered my roots and cleared them of weeds. In all the years I have been growing here, you never gave me a single drink."

Baba-Yaga ran to the gate. "Gate, gate!" she cried. "Did you lock her in?"

"No, I let her pass, for she greased my hinges. I served you for ever so long, but you never cared how I shrieked."

Baba-Yaga flew into a temper. She tried to break the gate but it flew back and knocked her down. She shook the birch tree but it lashed her with its branches. She beat the dog, but it bit her. She kicked the cat, but it scratched her. Tired and sore and bruised, she shook her fist at the forest and shouted, "Good riddance to you, Vasilisa. I'm better off without you." And then she greased the gate's hinges, watered the birch tree, threw a dog a bone and fed the cat some milk, and settled down to enjoy her dinner.

Meanwhile, Vasilisa ran through the forest till she had almost reached her home. Her steps slowed when she saw there was still no light on in the house. Her stepmother and stepsisters had been looking out for her, and now rushed out and began to chide and scold her.

"Stupid girl! What took you so long fetching the fire?" her stepmother demanded. "We have tried to strike a light again and again but to no avail. We have been so cold and hungry and afraid. Perhaps your fire will keep burning."

And the stepmother stepped forward and tried to seize the skull from Vasilisa. But its fiery eyes fixed themselves on her and her two daughters and burnt them like fire. The stepmother and her daughters screamed and tried to hide but, run where they would, the eyes followed them and never let them out of their sight 'til all three were burnt to cinders.

Vasilisa screamed with horror, but the burning eyes of the skull did not harm her. With shaking hands, she took out the little doll, and fed it a few crumbs and a thimbleful of milk. "Little doll, little doll, the fire I brought from Baba-Yaga has burned my stepmother and sisters to ashes. What should I do?"

"Bless them and bury them," the little doll said. "For they wanted you dead, but you are alive."

So Vasilisa gathered up the skull and the ashes, and buried them in the garden, saying a blessing in a shaking voice.

"Now, Vasilisa my dear, do not weep, but close your eyes and go to sleep. For morning is wiser than evening," the doll said.

The weary Vasilisa slept with the doll in her arms all night. In the morning she found a great bower of red roses growing on the spot where she had buried the skull and ashes.

Vasilisa's father soon came home. He was sorry to hear of the danger she had been in, but grateful that she had survived, with the help of her doll and her own quick wits. As for Vasilisa, she was overjoyed to have her father home safe again.

The years passed, and Vasilisa grew up, but the little wooden doll was never far from her. It was always glad to be fed a little bread and milk, and come to life and talk to her. In time, Vasilisa won the heart and the hand of the Tsar himself, and became known as Vasilisa the Wise for her goodness and kindness and cleverness.

But that is another story, to be told another time.

***

Kate Forsyth has written forty books, ranging from picture books to poetry, children's fantasy to historical novels for adults, and collections of essays and short stories. She has sold more than a million copies worldwide, been published in 17 languages, and won many awards including the 2015 American Library Association Award for Best Historical Fiction, the 2017 Aurealis Award for Best Collection, and the 2017 William Atheling Jr Award for Criticism. She is also an acclaimed speaker, performance storyteller and creative writing teacher, with a BA (Literature), a MA (Writing) and a Doctorate of Creative Arts.

A TALE SOON TOLD
Lissa Sloan

1.
Fair

The tale is soon told.

I have walked this path before. It winds through the wood, skirting gullies and rocky outcroppings, growing wide and narrow as it chooses. My feet know the way. They didn't to begin with, though. Not that first time, when they were bare and soft and felt the prick of every pine needle and pebble underneath them. Every part of me was soft then.

"Keep going," I breathed into the dark. All around me were the sounds of the wood at night. The hoot of an owl, the scratching of a mouse in the brush. The scream of a hare, a fox's teeth around its throat. The breeze rustled through the trees, and I pulled my shawl tighter around my shoulders. The spring days were getting warm, but the nights were cold still.

"Which way?" I whispered, as loud as I dared.

The voice came from the little doll clutched in my hand. *Between those trees, my love.*

"I cannot see the path," I whispered. "It is too dark."

To your right, dearest, she said. I held her up so her bright gaze fell on the trees she meant, lighting them just a little.

"It is too dark," I said again. "How could Anya see to make her lace in the dark?" I asked the doll. "Her pins make no light. She could see no better than me." She didn't answer. I kept walking.

I stumbled on a tree root, falling to my hands and knees. "And how could Olga see to knit?" I went on as I stood up, rubbing one stinging palm on my skirt. "Her needles make no light either. She could see no better than me." Then I added under my breath, "And I could see nothing."

My love, the doll said gently, *never mind your sisters now. You have your task, and you must do it. Do not worry tonight. The morning is wiser than the evening.* I knew she was right, so I said no more.

I went on through the forest. I walked a long time or a short time, the doll in my hand telling me to climb a rise or ford a stream or go straight ahead. And all the while I listened to the nighttime sounds of the wood: the howls and rustles, the creaks and shuffles.

At last I heard a new sound. It was the jingle of a horse's bridle, the muffled tread of hooves on the soft earth. I dropped the doll into my pocket and ducked behind a tree, my eyes fixed on the dark path before me. When the horse came through the trees, I saw her clearly. She almost glowed in the blackness, her mane streaming out behind her in the breeze. She was white. White like snow. White like the moon. White like new milk. And so was her rider. He was dressed all in white from his boots to his helmet.

The pair slowed on the path, and for a moment I forgot about my stepmother sending me to fetch fire from the baba yaga. I forgot my fear of the dark. I found myself stealing out from behind the tree, my hands searching my pockets until my fingers closed on what I wanted. It was one of the carrots I had stuffed into my pocket as I left the house. I wanted to give this beautiful creature something. I wanted to be near her warmth, to stand in her glow, if only for a moment. I took another step onto the path, holding out my offering.

The rider watched me. Perhaps he could see in the dark. Or perhaps his brightness illuminated everything around him. He stopped his horse and beckoned me closer, leaning down with his arms crossed on his horse's pommel. When the horse had accepted the carrot and moved on to nuzzling one of my braids, I heard a low chuckle. I looked up at the rider. His smile was warm, lifting his white mustaches at the edges and crinkling the corners of his eyes. He reached down and tapped my nose with one white-gloved finger. Then he winked, touched his mount with his heels, and the white horse and rider galloped away. The sky began to lighten. Dawn was coming at last.

The doll had told me that morning is wiser than evening; it was what she always said. I didn't feel any wiser, though. I began to see the wood around me as I walked. But I still needed the doll to tell me which way to go when the path forked or seemed to disappear entirely. I kept walking, a long time or a short time, listening to the birds waking and calling to each other in the growing light.

And then I heard the sound again; another horse was coming toward me through the trees. This time I wasn't so afraid. I only stepped off the path, but I didn't hide. Everything about this horse and rider was red. The horse's gleaming coat, her mane and tail, her saddle and bridle all were red. And so was her rider, from his cloak to the hair on his head. Red like apples. Red like poppies. Red like sweet peppers.

This rider slowed as the last one had, and I stepped forward, fumbling in my pocket for another carrot. The rider leaned back in his saddle, grinning, arms folded on his chest, as I offered my carrot. He was young. His horse was too, young and skittish. She flicked one ear, nervous, as she brought her mouth to my hand. Deciding I was harmless, she took the carrot, then tried to taste my fingers.

Just as I pulled my hand out of her reach, I felt a sharp tug on one of my braids. It hurt. Everything hurt me in those days. My stepmother always said I was tender-headed, as if it was a moral failing. I looked up, tears in my eyes, to see the rider straightening up in the saddle, holding his hands in the air as if to protest his innocence.

Should I smile or frown? Either way I was a fool, so I did neither. I only stepped out of his reach, protecting my braid with both hands. But I was foolish anyway. The red rider threw back his head and laughed, startling the birds in a nearby tree. Then he dug in with his red spurs and galloped away, laughing all the while. I could see the sun through a break in the trees now. It was day.

When it was fully light, I stopped walking. "It's morning," I said to the little doll. "Surely they won't need a light now. Perhaps I should turn back." I didn't whisper as I had in the dark, but still I spoke softly. My voice sounded odd among the other forest noises.

For a moment I thought the doll wouldn't answer. At last she said, *And what will happen if you return without it?* I knew the answer to her question: less food, more chores, maybe even my stepmother's birch rod across my back if my father wasn't home yet. I knew she was right, so I said no more. I walked on.

A long time or a short time, I walked. The sun changed position as it filtered through the new leaves, squirrels chattered and chased one another, magpies and thrushes flew from tree to tree. As the sunlight dimmed, turning everything to shades of blue and purple, I heard hoofbeats again. I stepped off the path and looked ahead, waiting for the next horseman to appear. I wondered what this one would be like. And I wondered why my heart was pounding in my chest.

The third horse and rider were black. Black like iron. Black like a starless sky. Black like when I closed my eyes in the dark. I had one more carrot in my pocket. Perhaps I would save this one, though, I thought as they came toward me. But the horse was so magnificent, its streaming mane glistening like a raven's wing, its eyes wild and shining. I found I had held out my carrot without even meaning to. My hand was trembling; I hoped the rider wouldn't see.

He was not smiling like the white rider, or laughing like the red. His face was serious, his black eyes meeting mine with some emotion I couldn't read. But it made my stomach jump into my throat. I wanted to back away and come closer all at once. I did neither, though. I stayed, frozen in place, as the black horse devoured my carrot and the rider bent down to me. He touched my chin with one black-gloved finger and leaned his face close to my ear. I thought he meant to whisper to me, but there were no words, only the warmth of his breath in my ear, the roughness of his stubble on my skin. And then for the briefest of moments his lips touched my cheek, burning through me like a fever.

I did back away then, one hand on my cheek. If I was trying to cure myself of that fever or to hold on to that feeling forever, I did not know. One corner of the black rider's lips turned up in the slightest of smiles, and I ran. Behind me, I heard the black horse's hoofbeats galloping away from me, and darkness descended upon the wood. Night had come.

It was too dark to run now. My hammering heartbeat eased, and my cheeks cooled as I slowed to a walk. I took a crumb of bread from my pocket and fed it to the little doll. "They say the baba yaga eats young girls," I said. "They say her teeth are made of iron, and her fingernails too. She flies through the wood in a mortar with a pestle in her hands." I don't know why I said these things. I was preparing myself, perhaps, for what was to come, for what was coming closer with every step. "They say her nose is so large it touches the ceiling of her hut when she sleeps at night. They say—"

My love, whispered the doll, gentle as always, *nothing will hurt you when I am with you. Do not think of these things tonight. Morning is wiser than evening.*

But I couldn't stop. "They say she lives in a hut that walks on chicken's legs. They say she has a fence, a fence—" I stopped, for I thought I could see a light on the path ahead. I took a few more steps through the thinning trees. "A fence made of bones." And I could see the bones now as I crept into the clearing: leg bones, arm bones, rib bones, all shining in the dark, lit by something on the fence posts. I thought I knew what the somethings were. "And on top of the fence posts," I whispered, "on top of the fence posts, there are skulls." And there were skulls, each one lit by a fire inside it which glowed red through its eyes and nose.

I stood at the edge of the clearing, gathering my courage. I breathed in and out. Once, twice, three times. I took one step, two steps, three. Then one of the skulls turned its fiery eyes in my direction. It began to scream. With that, all the other skulls faced me, and they screamed too. I clapped my hands to my ears, but that was the only move I could make. My feet were frozen to the forest floor. I couldn't even run. I could only stand and wait.

There was movement inside the fence of bones. By the light of the screaming skulls I could see the hut on chicken's legs. It was spinning and running around the tiny yard. From inside there was a crash and then a shout. "Be still!" At once, the giant legs stopped moving, and the door slammed open.

A figure stood silhouetted in the doorway, lit from inside. All I could see was her shape: wild hair, lumpy clothes, long-fingered hands with pointed nails. "What?" she demanded, her voice harsh. The skulls stopped screaming at once, turning their glowing eyes to her. "What is it?"

As one, the skulls all turned their fiery eyes on me. I threw up my hand to shield my eyes in the sudden brightness. The skull that had screamed first, the one on the gatepost, opened its jaw and spoke. "That," it crackled.

The figure slapped the wall of the hut with one hand, and the chicken legs bent, bringing the front of the house level with the ground. She stepped down and approached the gate, picking up the gatepost skull in one hand. She held it up, as if to get a better look at me. She crooked a bony, pointed finger, beckoning me to her. Now my legs moved, but I didn't want them to. They walked me straight up to the gate of bones.

I still could see nothing of her face but her eyes, which glowed red in the dark a little like the skulls. She now turned the skull to face her. "What is it?" she hissed.

The skull turned on her hand, its red gaze falling back on me. "What are you?"

I didn't know how to answer that question. "I…I…" I faltered.

Her voice was impatient. "Man, woman, beast? Russian?"

At last I said the obvious. "I'm a girl."

The figure before me held the skull close to my face, making it look me up and down. Then she leaned in and took a long, loud sniff. Her nose was impossibly big. "Girl? Hah!" she spat. "Not for long."

She was going to eat me. My legs began to shake. Desperation made me find my voice. "Please, grandmother," I burst out, "our fire has gone out, and my stepmother has sent me to fetch a light."

"Hah!" she said again, looking down at the skull, then back at me. "Come." She moved quickly for one so bent. She was through the doorway and the hut had risen back up before I had opened the gate. Then the hut turned its back on me, its chimney puffing smoke at an odd angle.

I walked through the gate and around to the door, but the door wasn't there anymore. For the house had started its mad spinning again. I tried calling to it. I tried to slap it as the baba yaga had, but I couldn't even get close.

So I shouted, my voice as loud as I could make it, "Little hut, little hut, turn your back to the forest and your front to me." That was what everyone said you should say, if you were foolish enough to want to enter the baba yaga's hut. The hut stopped, moving from side to side as if it were dizzy, then leaned down to let me up. I opened the door and stepped inside.

The hut was bigger than it looked from outside, the stove taking up one entire wall. Beside the fire, the baba yaga sat in a rocking chair, a stub-tailed tabby cat on her lap and a grizzled one-eyed hound at her feet. She grunted what might have been approval that I had managed to enter. Or perhaps it was disapproval; I couldn't tell.

"So," she barked. "You must fetch a light."

I nodded. "Yes, please, grandmother. My stepmother won't let me back in the house without one."

"Hah!" she sniffed. "Stepmother. I know her. And why you?"

I looked down. "My stepsisters—Anya said she could see to make her lace by the light of her pins, and Olga said she could see to knit by the light of her needles. But I couldn't see to spin."

There was a hiss as the old lady dumped the cat off her lap and crossed the room, stabbing one finger into my chest. "And you believed them, did you?"

"No," I shot back, stung. "Of course they couldn't see. Not any better than I could."

She looked down at me, tiny eyes bright in the firelight. "Well," she huffed. "You may not be a complete fool. So why you?"

I shrugged. "It's always me."

She lifted one bushy eyebrow. "They're jealous of your beauty, are they?"

I didn't know what to say to that. It was what the doll always said, but I wasn't sure I believed her. Anyway, the doll was a secret I wanted to keep, so I didn't mention her. "I don't know why they do it," I whispered to the floorboards.

She gave a shout of laughter. "Your humility, then?" She turned and walked back to her chair, waving a hand in the air, saying, "This is not trouble yet, my girl. You stay here and do some work for me. If you please me, I'll give you a light to take back home to those lying bitches." I choked down a laugh that threatened to escape. "If you don't…" she continued, studying me keenly. "Well, you look tender enough. We'll come to some arrangement. Now bring me my dinner, before I change my mind."

So I laid out the dinner that sat prepared on the stove: cabbage soup and black bread, roast hare and boar and pheasant, beer and wine and kvass. Enough to feed ten men. Once she had devoured all of it and climbed onto the flat top of the stove, she wrapped herself in blankets and was instantly asleep. I couldn't see if her enormous nose touched the ceiling, but surely it did. The sound of her snoring echoed around the hut.

I cleared away the dishes, giving the few bones the baba yaga had not eaten to the dog and cat. Then I crept into a corner and took the doll from my pocket. I offered her a crumb of black bread and a sip of soup, all that was left of the night's feast. As she ate, I whispered to her the impossible list of chores the baba yaga had given me for the next day. The sweeping, the cleaning, the weeding. The scouring, the sorting, the cooking. "If I don't do it," I breathed, "she will eat me. But how will I do it all, little doll?"

Rest, now, my love. All will be well. Morning is wiser than evening. Leave everything to me.

So I did, and all was well. For two days, the little doll and I did everything the baba yaga demanded. For two days we sorted and baked and cleaned and cooked. We did all the washing and pulled every weed in the yard. And we did it all under the glowing eyes of one of the fiery skulls. She had set it to watch us while she left and went about her mysterious work. It saw me stroking the scruffy cat and the flea-bitten dog and offering them scraps. It saw me feeding the little doll with crumbs of bread and asking her for advice.

For two days I saw the three horsemen ride by. I saw the white horseman before the dawn as the baba yaga rode out of her yard in her mortar and pestle. I saw the red horseman as the sun rose and the black horseman as it set, just before the baba yaga returned home. They were the same as when I met them on the forest path. The white rider gave me a friendly wave, and the red rider threw a pebble at the window to make sure I looked out. Then he galloped away laughing. The black rider did nothing; he only stared at me with that gaze that made me blush, though I didn't know why. I only knew I ran to the window when I heard his horse.

On the second morning, I woke before dawn to hear the baba yaga stretching and creaking on the stove. I sat up to stir the fire, but then I stopped, staring at the spot of red that bloomed on my skirt between my legs. There was a dull ache in my lower belly. My heart thrummed in my ears, and I went cold with fear.

"I told you," she said from behind me. She had climbed down from the stove while I sat dumbly on the floor.

I looked up, not understanding. "Will I die?"

She snorted, dropping a basket beside me. "Not today." She rolled her beady eyes at my stupidity. "I said you would not be a girl much longer. You are a woman." Then she began to laugh as she walked away. "This is not trouble yet."

The door slammed behind her, and I looked in the basket. It was full of clean rags. At last I understood. My stepsisters had a basket like this, and I often had to wash their bloody rags myself. I had long put up with their taunts that I was not a woman as they were. Now I was.

That night when the baba yaga came in, her red eyes roamed the hut just as it had the night before. When she could find no fault with the state of it, she whirled on her fiery skull. "What has she gotten up to while I was away?"

"She has been at work, my mistress," rasped the skull. "As you see." The baba yaga turned away from it with a huff, taking another look around the room. The glow in one of the skull's eyes went out for a moment, making a fiery wink at me. "She is a hard worker. And she is kind."

"Kind?" the old lady barked. "What good is kind?"

I sometimes wondered that myself, when my father was away and I was alone with my stepmother and stepsisters. But kind had been good enough to win the skull's silence, I supposed.

The baba yaga approached me and poked me in the chest with one iron claw. "I am not kind. I am hungry."

I took a deep breath. "Sit down, then, grandmother. Your supper is ready."

The old lady smacked and crunched and sucked down the feast I had prepared for her, enough to feed twenty men. At last, wiping a hand across her greasy chin, she turned her eyes on me. "Aren't you curious about anything you see here, my girl? Why don't you ever ask me anything?"

I would be lying to pretend I wasn't curious, and so I asked. "Who is the white horseman, grandmother?"

She leaned one hand down, letting the one-eyed dog lick her fingers. "The horsemen are my servants," she said, a bit of a smirk on her withered lips. She was proud of these uncanny men who did her bidding. "He is my bright dawn. You know him."

I nodded. I didn't really know him, but he felt familiar somehow. The baba yaga looked at me expectantly, so I dared to ask her another question. "Who is the red horseman, grandmother?"

She smiled indulgently. "He is my red sun. You know him."

I nodded again. The red horseman too, felt like someone I knew, even though he wasn't really.

She was watching me keenly now. She knew the next question on my lips just as well as I did. But if I wanted my answer, I would have to say the words. "And grandmother, who is the black horseman?" I said at last.

There was something secretive in her expression. "He is my dark night," she said, her eyes searching mine. "You know him?" This time it was a question. I shook my head. She leered at me. "You will, my girl. You will." I blushed, though I still did not know why. Then she burst into a bawdy laugh, showing her mouth full of iron teeth. Still laughing, she left the table and made her way to the chair beside the fire. "And now," she said, beckoning to me, "I have a question for you."

I came over. "Yes, grandmother?" My hand closed around the doll in my pocket, hoping her touch would give me comfort.

"How can you do all the tasks I give you? You know they are impossible."

I did know that, yet the doll had helped me finish them all. My mouth went dry. "I...I..." I slipped the doll behind my back, shielding her from the witch's anger. "I have something to help me," I said at last.

She leaned forward in her chair, a bit of spittle on her wrinkled lip. "What?"

"It is...it is my mother's blessing," I managed at last. It was true enough.

"Blessing?" The baba yaga shot out of her chair. "Get out! I'll have no blessed creatures in my house." She backed me toward the door, which flew open as we drew near. The house tilted wildly and I fell, dropping the doll and barely managing to hold onto the door frame.

The old lady seemed to have no trouble keeping her balance. She stooped down and picked up the doll, then turned her pitiless eyes on me. I hung in the doorway, my legs dangling above the yard and my fingers reddening with the strain. "This is not trouble yet," she said, her eyes burning angrily. "Trouble is before you, my girl. Such trouble that mere blessings will not be enough. You must have something more." She held up the doll. "Even your *blessing* knows that, and if she won't admit it, she is a bigger fool than you." With that, she threw the little doll out the door.

My grip on the door frame faltered, and I fell to the yard below, my hands full of splinters. She slammed the door, and the eyes of all the skulls on the fence posts turned to me as I got to my feet. Then the door reopened, and something round came hurtling out the door. It hit me hard in the stomach, knocking me back to the ground. "Take your light, if you must have it," came her voice from above me. "Give it to your stepmother, with my compliments." I staggered to my feet, looking at the round ball in my hands. It was the fiery skull.

I found the doll, lying next to me in the yard. I picked her up and put her in my pocket. "Thank you, grandmother," I panted, when I could get my breath back.

"Don't thank me!" she screeched as I reached the gate. "And remember what I said."

I nodded, closing the gate of bones behind me. I would remember. "This is not trouble yet," I whispered to myself as I stepped out of the clearing. I held the fiery skull in front of me to light my way. It turned to me and seemed to grin.

"I will need something more."

2.
Brave

The tale is soon told, but the journey is long.

The next time I walked this path, I did need something more. My feet were not so soft this time, and they were not bare. I wasn't wearing the fine embroidered slippers I had grown used to wearing either, or any of the elegant things my lover brought me. My shoes were made of iron. I had forged them myself: three pairs, just as I had been told. They were hard and unyielding, and my feet were covered in blisters. I was no longer so raw that everything hurt me, but I still had softness enough.

The leaves were the deep green of summer now; they shaded me from the heat of the sun. I didn't come into the wood for a light this time. I cared only for the bright falcon feathers dropping from the sky, and the trail they made for me to follow. But my feet knew the way the feathers led, down the path as it wound through the wood, skirting gullies and rocky outcroppings, growing wide and narrow as it chose. It seemed familiar now.

And the horsemen, when I saw them, looked just the same. The white rider stopped and extended his hand. When I put my hand in his, he squeezed it, patting it with his other hand, a smile curving his mustaches just as it had done before.

The red rider stopped too. He leaned down from the saddle, beckoning me close as if to tell me something. Then he made a rude noise with his tongue and gave my ear a quick tug. It didn't hurt this time; I only smiled and wiped the spit off my face as he sat back up with a grin. Then he was off, his laughter fading into the brightening day.

The black rider reached for my hand as the white rider had. Our eyes met as he turned my hand over and kissed my palm. The baba yaga had said I would know him, and now I did. At least I knew what that look meant, the one that had made me blush. I had seen it in the eyes of Finist the Falcon on those moonlit nights when he flew in my window. When he changed into a handsome young man before my eyes.

I cannot say how long I walked; it was a long time or a short time. But after a while the feathers led me to the clearing I remembered so well. The hut scratched at the earth inside its fence of bones, and as I came through the trees, my iron staff broke in two. By the light of the fiery skulls I looked down at my feet. I held one of them up to see that the soles of my iron shoes had worn away completely. And I knew I had choked down the last bite of my stone church wafer not an hour before.

I had two more iron staves to break, two more pairs of iron shoes to wear out, and two more church wafers to gnaw through before I could see Finist the Falcon again. I had walked so far and so long, with nothing to show for it but a pocket full of feathers. And still I had so far to go. I swayed there, not sure how I could take another step. Perhaps I would have stayed there all night if I hadn't heard the screaming. The fiery skulls had seen me.

As before, the hut began to spin, and as before, a voice shouted, "Be still!" And the hut was still. The baba yaga appeared in her doorway and came out as the hut bent to let her down. She, too, was the same. At least I thought she was. My legs shook, but with weariness, not terror, as I watched her hobble to the gate. Maybe I was the different one.

The old lady picked up the skull on the gatepost. "What is it?"

The skull turned its grinning face to me. "What are you?"

I thought I knew the answer to the question this time. "I am a woman," I said.

The baba yaga sighed in exasperation, turning from me to her skull. "Maiden, lover, mother?"

Well, I was no maiden. And why was I here, if not to find my love? This, then, was the answer. "Lover."

The baba yaga leaned her long nose close to me and gave me a noisy sniff. She made a huffing noise. "Not for much longer."

I looked at her, not understanding. She couldn't mean Finist the Falcon no longer loved me. And she couldn't mean he was dead. I would not accept either possibility. I said nothing; I only looked at her, waiting for her to explain.

She sighed again, resigned to my stupidity, or my presence. Or perhaps both. "Come in, then."

This time she let me cross the threshold with her. She pointed to two chairs beside the enormous stove. There had only been one there before. "Sit," she commanded. I sat. Sleeping in the glow of the fire were the same stub-tailed cat and one-eyed hound. It had not been so many years since I had been here, but the animals had seemed old even then.

The baba yaga was bustling about, and after a moment I turned to see what she was doing. She was filling two tea cups from an ornate samovar. It seemed an odd thing to find in such a humble hut. But the tea, when she pressed the warm cup into my hands, smelled delicious. She sat across from me with a cup of her own, her eyes fixed on me. "Drink," she demanded. I drank.

"Thank you, grandmother," I said when the tea was gone, forgetting she didn't like to be thanked.

She scowled. "Well?" she said, waiting to hear my story.

So I told it. I told her how my father had brought me the feather of Finist the Falcon. And how the falcon had flown in through my window and transformed into a handsome prince. How he had wooed me and won my heart. How my stepsisters became suspicious that I had a secret visitor every night.

"Stepsisters," the baba yaga sniffed. "I know them."

I told her how they had drugged my drink so I fell asleep waiting for my lover, and how they had closed my window. How they had lined it with knives and needles to cut the falcon's breast as he beat his bright wings at the glass.

She held up a gnarled hand, fingers warped and joints swollen. "Wait. Why did my light not take care of these stepsisters of yours? It should have."

"It did," I said. Her fiery skull had burned my stepmother and stepsisters to ashes. It had burned our house to the ground. She was watching me for an explanation, bushy brows raised. "I have new stepsisters. My father married again."

"Hah!" she spat. Then she shook her head. "Father. I know him." She stood up and led me to the table. It was not enough food for twenty men, or even ten, but after all that time in the forest, it was a feast to me.

When we had finished nearly all of it and laid a plate of scraps on the floor for the dog and the cat, I asked the baba yaga the question I couldn't get out of my mind. "Grandmother," I said, "what you said before, what did you mean?" She seemed to know what I meant, about me not being a lover for much longer, but she just sat, fingering a wart on her chin. I would have to say it myself, I supposed. "Did you mean he doesn't love me?"

She shrugged. "Is it true love? That's up to you and your falcon." She looked me up and down. "It's not those church wafers making you plump."

Her last statement made no sense, so I ignored it. "But grandmother, I am so tired. He said I wouldn't see him again until I broke three iron staves, wore out three pairs of iron shoes, and gnawed through three stone church wafers. He said I must travel three times nine tsardoms from my home. I don't know how I will ever find him."

She sat back in her chair with a sniff. "And where is your *blessing* now?"

I looked down at my hands. "I lost her," I whispered. I didn't know when it had happened, or how. Maybe I had a hole in my pocket that I didn't know about, and the little doll fell out. I had gone so long without needing her, without even thinking about her. But one day, I did need her. I reached for her, and she was gone.

I expected the baba yaga to gloat, but she didn't laugh or even smile. She just nodded, her beady eyes shiny. They didn't look red at all. "It happens that way," she said roughly.

"But now I need her, and I don't know what to do next."

The old woman stood up, put her clawed hands on my shoulders, and pulled me to my feet. I hadn't grown much since the last time, but she seemed smaller now. "Next, you will go to sleep," she said sharply, taking my chin in her fierce grip. "And in the morning, you will get up." She stabbed my chest with a finger on each of the last four words.

With that, she threw a blanket at me and turned to climb up on the stove. She mumbled something as I spread the blanket before the fire. Her voice was so soft I barely heard it, but as I lay down to sleep, her words echoed in my ears. *Morning is wiser than evening.*

I felt no wiser in the morning, but I got up. The baba yaga was bustling about, laying black bread and honey on the table. She poured two cups of tea from her samovar, and we sat down.

"Now," she said as we ate, "I know your falcon. He is to marry the daughter of a tsar who lives three times six tsardoms from here. That is all I know, but perhaps my grandmother will know more. You go see her and ask her."

I stared at her in disbelief. "Just follow the path," she said, apparently thinking nothing of that fact that her grandmother must be impossibly old.

"Yes, grandmother," I said, standing up from the table and taking out the second pair of iron shoes from my pack.

"Take this," she said, pushing a gnarled hand under my nose. In it was a fine spindle, made of silver. Like the samovar, it was a thing of beauty that seemed to have no place here.

"Thank you," I said, taking it. "Is this the thing I will need? You told me I would need something more."

She made a huffing sound. "I can't give you that." She crossed her arms, her eyes still on me. "But you might find that little trinket useful. It will spin gold thread." Her look had turned crafty, cunning. "Perhaps you can give it to your falcon's bride as a wedding present. If you get there in time." There was a challenge in her eyes.

I stuffed the spindle in my pack. "I will do no such thing," I said, and put my feet into the new iron shoes as she crowed with laughter.

"She'll do well," she said to the fiery skull on the table.

Together we walked out the door and into the yard. At the gate made of bones I stopped and turned around. I opened my mouth to ask a question, but nothing came out. I didn't know what to ask.

Her eyes narrowed, and she reached out a clawed hand to touch my face. "This is not trouble yet, my girl," she said, her hand resting on my cheek. Then she gave me a light slap. "Not yet." With that, she turned and went back into the hut, her cackle following her inside.

And I began to walk. I walked a long time or a short time, turning her words over and over in my mind. One thing in particular kept coming back to me. *It's not those church wafers making you plump.* It made no sense, I thought to myself one day as I rummaged in my pack for the second stone wafer. It had fallen to the bottom, in among my little stock of rags. I hadn't needed them at all on this journey, I realized.

Time was strange here in the wood. It was summer. It had been the whole time, and the seasons showed no sign of changing. Had I been here a short time or a long time? I didn't know, but I had seen the moon wax and wane several times as I walked through those long summer nights. I had seen three full moons at least. Maybe four. And all that time I had not bled. She said I was growing plump. *Maiden? Lover? Mother?* She said I would not be a lover much longer. Perhaps she meant not only a lover.

I didn't know for certain she was right, but I began to suspect. And by the time I reached the baba yaga's grandmother's hut, I knew she was. My pains had begun hours before, and now I couldn't go another step. My second iron staff snapped in two, and I sank down in front of another gate of bones.

The skulls on these fence posts did not scream in warning, though; they merely seemed to hum. Before long, I felt brittle fingers closing around my shoulders, lifting me up. A fleshy arm, surprising in its strength, came around my waist and led me inside another chicken-legged hut.

It was as if the old grandmother had been expecting me. There was a pile of blankets spread out beside the stove, and bottles of herbs and potions were laid out nearby. She drew me in, letting me stop when I needed to, and settled me on the blankets. Then she put a cup of wine in my hands. "Drink," she said, her voice rough. "It will help."

The wine was bitter with the concoction of herbs in it, but I drank. Only then did I look at the old baba yaga's face. She was every bit as fierce as her granddaughter: wild hair, warts, and all, and even more wrinkled. But I didn't even think to be frightened of her. As my body prepared to split itself in two, I had other things to fear.

But the old grandmother was with me the entire time, rubbing her gnarled fingers into my back or offering me willow bark to ease the pain. She did not mind if I cried or screamed or dug my nails into her arms as my body went about its work. "This is not trouble yet," she crooned into my ear, almost a song. And when the pain was so bad I could not bear it, she said it again. And I bore it. I had no other choice. Again and again she said it, until what was one became two. Her hands were gentle as they cradled my child and brought her to my breast at last.

It was only when we were tucked up comfortably beside the stove, my pain beginning to be forgotten, that I thought to look around me. The hut was the same as the first baba yaga's, except for little differences. There was a stub-tailed cat and a one-eyed dog, but the cat was a different color, and the dog's hair was longer. There was an elegant samovar, but it had a different shape.

As the old grandmother dished out a bowl of porridge and poured a cup of tea from the samovar, I told her of where I had been and where I was going. When I was finished, I looked down at the face of my daughter. She was strangely wizened, like an old grandmother herself. She fixed me with a hard, almost bitter stare. Her look was full of questions, full of expectations, full of demands. She seemed like no one I recognized. And now this bitter stranger must come with me, to a faraway tsardom to meet her father. If I could ever find him.

My cheeks were wet with tears I didn't remember shedding. "Grandmother," I whispered, "I don't know how to go on."

She took the baby from me, nestling her in one arm as she handed me a bowl of porridge and a spoon. Then she sat across from me, rocking in her chair. "I will tell you," she said, her voice soft, but crackling like the fire. "Tonight, you will go to sleep. And in the morning, you will get up." She stopped rocking and leaned forward in her chair. "And then you will take one step. And another, and another."

So I went to sleep. In the morning, we ate black bread with honey and drank more tea from the samovar. When we were finished, the old baba yaga said, "I know your falcon. He is to marry the daughter of a tsar who lives three times three tsardoms from here. Perhaps you will find him before the wedding." She rubbed her nose, thinking. It was a big nose, but maybe not big enough to touch the ceiling. "That is all I know, but perhaps my grandmother will know more. You go see her and ask her."

I should have been surprised, that there was a woman in this world even older than this old grandmother, but I only nodded. "Yes, grandmother," I said and looked around for my iron shoes. I didn't remember taking them off the night before, but my feet were bare now.

The old grandmother waved a wrinkled hand toward the window. I looked out. Outside the fence of bones were the remains of my second pair of iron shoes. The soles were worn through. I remembered now that I had chewed through the last bit of the second stone church wafer the day before. I opened my pack for the third pair of shoes.

The baba yaga had been rummaging in a trunk and now brought me what she had found: some garments for the baby and spare cloth to strap her to my back. Then she drew out two more things: a golden platter and a silver ball. Like the silver spindle, these seemed like a magical gift.

"Thank you, grandmother," I said. She made a grumble of disapproval at my thanks. "Are these what I will need? The something more?"

She gave a snort of laughter. "I cannot give you that," she said. "That is inside you already." Then she gave me a sly smile. "But you might make use of these. Perhaps you could give them to your falcon's bride as a wedding present."

I almost laughed. "I will give her nothing," I said, opening my pack and putting the platter and ball inside.

She winked at me and grinned, multiplying the wrinkles around her eyes. "See that you don't."

We parted at the gate of bones. I took one step, just as she had said I should, but then I turned back. This old lady was round where her granddaughter was bony; the lines of her face were softer. But the look she gave me was every bit as fierce. "This is not trouble yet," she said.

I nodded. "Not yet," I repeated. I turned and took one step, and another, and another. Soon, my second pair of ruined iron shoes was behind me.

And I walked. It was a long time or a short time, though it was always summer in the wood. Frogs croaked, insects buzzed, and the sun poured in lazily through the leaves. The little stranger strapped to my back became familiar to me, and soon I wondered if there had ever been a time when she wasn't with me. And yet I knew no more than I had before. Why would she not sleep in the few hours when I stopped at night, too tired to continue? Why did she arch her back and turn her face from my breast? Why did she fix me with that bitter stare I couldn't understand? Most of all, why did she cry so much?

I called my bitter daughter Masha, and whether she cried or slept or didn't sleep, I walked. I put one foot in front of the other, again and again and again. And when I arrived in front of the next hut on chicken's legs, Masha was crying again. It was night. She had cried all day and kept rubbing her face with one tiny fist. This hut, too, was surrounded by a fence of bones, but the fiery skulls on the fence posts didn't scream when I approached. They opened their jaws and wailed, singing along with my daughter's cries.

The hut's door slammed open, and the oldest grandmother squinted down at us. She crooked her finger at me to come closer, so I came through the gate and stood in the pool of light cast from inside the hut. She tilted her grizzled head and motioned for me to turn around. When I had made a full circle, she spoke. "Babies. Hah. Little nuisances, aren't they?" She walked back inside, leaving the door open. The hut bent down to let me in, and I walked inside.

I tested my last iron staff before leaning it in a corner by the door. It felt as though it might break, but it didn't. I set my pack down by the stove, hearing the clunk of the last church wafer inside as the pack hit the floor. I unstrapped my daughter; it had been awkward at first, but the movements came easily to me now. The oldest baba yaga, tiny and wizened, sat in one of the chairs beside the fire and clapped her papery hands impatiently, holding them out for the baby.

"Give it here," she commanded.

I handed over the wailing child and sat, looking down at my last pair of iron shoes. The soles were thin, but not worn through. Like the staff and the stone wafer, there was some life left in them. My journey was not over, and I was afraid. Afraid they would never wear out, afraid they would and I still wouldn't find my love. Afraid I didn't have the strength to take another step.

Across from me, the old lady was holding my daughter up at arm's length, and they studied one another in silence. Masha had stopped crying and merely stared at the wrinkled face before her: the wild white hair, the single hair sprouting from the pointed chin. "Hmm," the grandmother said at last, tucking the baby into the crook of her arm and beginning to rock. The child stuffed a fist into her mouth and began to whine.

The baba yaga slid a finger into Masha's mouth, feeling for something, then shot her a sour look when the child bit down. "Hmm," she said again, and reached behind her for a bottle of brown liquid as the baby opened her mouth and began to scream again. Uncorking the bottle, she dribbled a little on her finger and put it into Masha's now open mouth, rubbing it on the tiny pink gums. Almost at once, the screaming stopped.

"Hah!" the oldest grandmother crowed, triumphant.

"How…" I breathed, not able to finish my question. Masha never stopped crying like that for me.

The baba yaga leaned forward, guiding my finger into the child's mouth. There on the gums, where it was smooth before, there was something rough under the surface. "A tooth," she said, her mouth splitting into a wide grin. She had hardly any teeth herself, and they weren't iron, or even pointed.

I had known nothing about babies before I had my own, and in the forest, there had been no one to teach me. All I knew I had discovered for myself. But there was so much I didn't know. How would I ever learn it all?

"You too?" she said. I looked into the baba yaga's wrinkled face. I didn't know what she meant, until she reached into a pocket and handed me a threadbare handkerchief. My cheeks were wet with hot tears, and now they were flowing, I didn't think they would ever stop.

Masha had fallen asleep. As I cried, the old woman tucked her into a basket beside the stove. Then she began to lay the table for supper. A stub-tailed cat hopped into my lap, butting its head against my face, and a one-eyed hound forced its cold nose into my hand. At last, my tears slowed to a trickle.

"Finished?" the baba yaga asked. I nodded. She motioned me over to the table and sat down across from me. "Well?" she said, waiting to hear my story. Over cabbage soup and black bread, and tea from yet another ornate samovar, I told her everything. I told her where I had been and where I was going.

"I don't know how to go on, grandmother," I finished, "and I am afraid."

I waited for her to tell me this is not trouble yet, but she didn't. She snorted out a laugh. "Of course you are afraid," she said. "You'd be a fool if you weren't." She sat back in her chair, lighting a pipe. "This is what you will do," she said, smoke curling around her face and into the wisps of her hair. "Tonight, you will go to sleep. In the morning, you will get up. You will take one step, and another, and another." Her bony finger reached across the table, landing between my breasts. "And you will go on." With each word, she poked me in the heart. It was not a claw, not a talon. Her nails were long, thick, and discolored, but they weren't made of iron.

She threw me a bundle of quilts and gestured to a spot by the stove. "Go on now," she said. "Morning is wiser than the evening." She leaned back in her chair with a laugh that became a phlegmy cough and then a laugh again.

In the morning, Masha's first tooth had broken through her gums. She sucked on a piece of black bread as the baba yaga and I had our bread and honey. After taking a drink of her tea, the oldest grandmother fixed me with beady eyes. "Now," she said. "I know your falcon. He is to marry the daughter of a tsar who lives in the next tsardom. The wedding is three days from tomorrow. You can still get there in time."

I nodded. "Thank you, grandmother." She made a rude noise with her tongue, and I picked up my third pair of iron shoes. There was life in them yet, maybe just the amount I needed. I strapped my daughter to my back and leaned down to pick up my pack. The oldest grandmother appeared at my side. "You might need this," she said, holding out the bottle of brown liquid she had used on Masha's gums. "And you might as well take this." She held out a golden embroidery frame. In it was a piece of fine linen with a needle stuck into it. "The needle sews by itself," she explained. She said it proudly, as if she had created it herself.

I thanked her. I knew this would not be the *something more* I needed. That was within me, the last baba yaga had said. This baba yaga went on, "It is a pretty thing. Perhaps you could give it to your falcon's bride. She's just like a magpie, you know, collecting a nest full of pretty things. Like your falcon." She said it softly, not goading, not challenging, just thoughtful. I was silent. I would give this tsar's daughter nothing. Nothing without something in return, anyway. And what if there were something this princess wanted even more than my falcon? Perhaps these gifts would be valuable after all.

The old lady followed me out of the hut to the fence of bones. At the gate we both stopped, and she trailed one finger over Masha's cheek. "Nuisance," she said, before planting a kiss on the top of her head. Then she came around to me. I looked down at her, waiting for her to speak, but she said nothing. Perhaps I must say it for myself, I thought. "This is not trouble yet," I said.

She snorted. In her eyes, there was a flicker of red—now there, then gone. "Life is trouble, my girl."

I nodded. Life is trouble. I turned and took one step, and another, and another. And I went on.

3.
Wise

The tale is soon told, but the journey is long. And it is not over yet.

I have walked this path before. It winds through the wood, skirting gullies and rocky outcroppings, growing wide and narrow as it chooses. But it is different these days. Some old trees have cracked, died, or lost limbs. A boulder or two has rolled down and into the path. The stream has changed its course here and there. But still it is familiar. My feet know the way.

They are not bare this time, or clad in iron shoes. I am not wearing finely embroidered slippers either, as I once did. I cannot tolerate such flimsy things now. My toenails are becoming thick and sharp. My feet are bony and wide. I need the protection of strong tanned calfskin on the outside and the softness of sheepskin within. My boots are not ornate or beautiful, but I don't need such things anymore. Besides, it is autumn now. The path beneath my feet is covered with leaves of red, brown, and gold, and the wind blows in sharp gusts. Winter will be here soon.

I have been walking this path a long time or a short time. In truth, it has been a long time. I know that. And sometimes it feels that way, when my joints creak and my muscles ache and the cold creeps into my bones. Everything hurts, most days. But more than anything it feels like a short time. And when I see my reflection in the stream, I barely recognize the woman floating there. My breasts have fallen and my waist has risen. I have too much hair where I shouldn't and not enough where I should. How did I get so gray, and when did my cheeks grow so wrinkled? Has so much time really passed?

When the horsemen appear on the path, I see they haven't

changed at all. Not to look at, anyway. But something is different. The white rider greets me with a warm smile, and once he is past me, he stops. He holds his hand out, offering to pull me up behind him. I shake my head without quite knowing why. I only know I am not ready to go with him. Not yet. He nods acceptance. Perhaps he will make the offer again next time we meet. He rides away.

I only glimpse the red rider through the trees. He seems to be riding along a different path, one I don't quite know how to reach. He raises a hand and waves, craning his neck to get a look at me through the trees. But his horse seems to carry him away without his intending her to. I blink, and he is gone, his laughter fading away on the chill wind.

The black rider is on my path, but he does not stop. He doesn't look my way. In fact, I don't think he sees me at all. I am used to that by now. I am used to all sorts of looks. The looks of pity, of derision, of sickening sweetness, as if I were a child again. The looks of amusement or mockery. I am laughable, I know. But mostly, I am used to no looks at all.

What does it matter? I have no need of a man to look at me the way the horseman in black did once. My falcon gazed at me that way too. But he has flown away again, to a country farther than the farthest sea, farther than the farthest mountains. Farther than nine times nine times nine tsardoms. There are not enough iron shoes in this wide world to lead me to him now. I cannot follow him where he has gone. Not yet, anyway.

I walk on. As I near the clearing where the hut on chicken's legs used to stand, I find I am whispering to myself. "They say the old baba yaga is dead," I say. "They say no one has seen her for years. They say there never was such a woman in the first place. Riding through the forest in a mortar," I tell myself. "It's preposterous."

But I refuse to believe my own whispers. For how could she be dead? How could she be gone when I hear her voice so clearly? At times when trouble opens its maw to swallow me whole, she is so close I feel her hot breath in my ear. Times like now. *Get up*, she tells me every morning. *Take a step, and another, and another. Go on.* And so I do.

When I reach the clearing at last, I see it is all still there. I was afraid it would have vanished. So afraid I almost sob with relief, but I am dry. Everything may hurt nowadays, but I rarely shed tears. I merely stand, leaning on my thick staff, oak this time, not iron, and drink in every detail. The hut stands on one taloned foot; the other is tucked up underneath it, as if it is sleeping. But there is a light within. The mortar and pestle are in one corner of the yard. The fence of bones is there too.

Perhaps it is my fading sight, but the light in the fiery skulls doesn't glow like it used to. At least, not until they see me. I wince, waiting for the scream. But they don't scream. The lights in their eye sockets grow brighter and slowly dim to black. Then the eyes light up again, bright and welcoming. They are like a group of contented cats, blinking at a friend. They don't scream, so I dare to come close.

When I reach the gate, the skull on the gatepost speaks. "What are you?" it crackles. Its voice is familiar.

After all this time, I suppose I should know the answer it is looking for, although I never seem to. I am no girl, no maiden. I was a lover, once. The old woman had said it would be up to me and my falcon, if it was true love. And once I had broken the spell of the magpie princess, we made it true. It wasn't always easy; we had trouble enough. But life is trouble, and we faced it together. There were other children after Masha, a boy and another girl. After my falcon's father died, the whole tsardom was ours, through bad fortune and good, famine and plenty. But my Finist is gone, and I will never be a lover again.

And am I a mother? Not to my bitter Masha, for she is gone as well. She flew to her father, taking her baby with her. I should have gone first, but I remain. A leftover. I do have my other children, my Ivan and my Irina. But they are grown. My Ivan is tsar now; my Irina is married to a faraway prince with children of her own. Babies. They have no need of me.

Daughter, sister, friend. All these roles are fading too, as others leave before me to that unknown country. I have no wish to take any of the names left to me: dowager tsarina, unwanted houseguest, object of pity. Nuisance.

This is my trouble. I get up every day; I take one step, and another, and another. I go on, just as she told me. And perhaps she would tell me all of this is not trouble. But I cannot rid myself of the feeling that only she would understand me now.

I don't know what answer the fiery skull wants this time. Maybe I don't care. I look down into its flaming eyes. "I am myself."

The lights in its eyes go out and come back, a blink of assent. The gate of bones swings open. The hut seems to wake, but it doesn't run or spin. The tucked leg drops to the ground, and the hut tilts to the side, as if it were looking at me through its window-eyes. Then it bows down to let me in, its door falling open. I pick up the skull and take it with me to light my way.

"Grandmother?" I call, stepping in. My voice is creaky and thin. The door closes behind me, and I grab onto the latch for balance as the hut raises back up to standing. There is another slight shift of the floor. Perhaps the hut has drawn up one foot to go back to sleep. But I don't see its mistress anywhere. Perhaps she is outside somewhere nearby.

I can wait. I set the fiery skull down on the table and look around me. The hut is much the same as it always has been. I poke around, lifting the lids of the pots of meat and soup and porridge. I am so hungry. I could eat enough to feed ten men. The ornate samovar is there in its old place. There is one chair, inhabited by a stub-tailed cat, and a scruffy dog sleeps on the rug below it. The dog opens its one eye and thumps its tail, but it doesn't get up. The basket of rags is in one corner. I have no need of those now. I am dry.

With some difficulty, I climb to the top of the stove, fearing what

I might find there. Perhaps she is ill. Perhaps she is dead. But the ledge above the stove is empty. It is warm there, and soft with all those blankets. I am so tired. I am always tired these days. Everything hurts.

I climb down. The fiery skull watches me, just as it did the first time I came here. But if it thinks I am doing something wrong, it says nothing. I look around me, unsure of what to do next. What if she never comes back? I am afraid.

I sigh and lower myself into the chair. The cat hops down with a hiss. I am a fool, but I will wait for her. There is food here, and a warm bed. If she doesn't come soon, perhaps I will eat something. And then, if she still doesn't come, perhaps I will crawl up onto the stove and sleep. I can decide what to do in the morning. Morning is wiser than evening, after all.

The dog settles its head on my feet with a sleepy groan, and the cat jumps into my lap. She kneads my thighs and belly, making a comfortable spot. I have padding enough for that. Something digs into my leg. There is something in my pocket, a little lump. I reach my hand in to draw it out.

It is a doll, my little doll. I know that cannot be. She fell out of my pocket so long ago. And yet here she is, just the same, maybe a little smaller than before. I don't imagine if I fed her a crumb of bread and a sip of tea that she would open her eyes and speak to me the way she used to. But it is good to see her all the same. After all this time. I reach into another pocket for a handkerchief to wipe my eyes. It is true that I am dry these days, but sometimes my old body leaks. Just a bit.

A long time or a short time I wait. I doze in the warmth of the fire, the doll clasped in my hand. The screams wake me. The skulls outside are screaming, and the house begins to spin. The baba yaga must be home at last. But she doesn't stop the hut, and the scream of the skulls goes on and on. I am dizzy, and my ears ring with the noise.

I stomp one boot on the floor. "Be still!" I shout.

There is silence, and the house stops moving, swaying a bit for a moment before it is finally still. But it doesn't lean down to let its mistress in. I lean forward, peering out the window into the dark. All I can see is a small figure outside the gate.

I look over at the fiery skull. It is looking out the window too. "What is it?" I ask.

It turns to me. "Let's ask it," it says.

As I stand and walk to the window, I hear a voice calling. I cannot pick out all it says, only two words: *grandmother* and *trouble*. I see her now, standing at the fence, terror in her eyes. It is a girl. Not for much longer, though. She will be a woman soon. But for now, she is fair and soft and foolish. I know her.

I slide the doll back into my pocket. This girl does not know trouble. Not yet. Trouble is before her. And when she meets it, she will need something more. I cannot give it to her, or even tell her what it is. She will have to find it on her own. But it is so very dark, and she looks so very cold. I walk toward the door.

My feet know the way.

***

Lissa Sloan's poems and short stories are published in *Enchanted Conversation, Krampusnacht: Twelve Nights of Krampus,* and *Frozen Fairy Tales.* "Death in Winter," Lissa's contribution to *Frozen Fairy Tales,* was nominated for a Pushcart Prize. Visit her at her website, lissasloan.com, or on Twitter: @LissaSloan.

BABA YAGA: HER STORY
Jill Marie Ross

In the old country, many years ago—so long ago that the stories have become legends—there lived a woman of the forest. She lived a lonely, bitter existence. She was reviled by the country folk, who told stories of terrible, horrible deeds done by her. Some had truth behind them, for the woman known as Baba Yaga was certainly no angelic creature. Let us start at the beginning, and then you will know about this Baba Yaga, and you can decide for yourself about her.

See a small girl, a girl with no name, thin and dressed in ragged clothes, hiding among the pine trees near a small clearing. This girl had no place to call home other than the forest and the mountains behind them, with all their thickets and caves, nooks and crannies. She spent hours crouched in hiding places near the village and the outlying huts, watching other children, always watching. She watched them play their games and share their secrets. She saw them help each other sometimes and hurt each other sometimes, too. She stole scraps of food from rubbish heaps and produce from gardens when she could, but most of her time was spent watching and learning, watching and longing. For this girl was the loneliest creature in the forest.

The rest of her time was spent roaming through the trees, crawling through the thickets, picking her way up the mountains, always followed by birds and the small animals of the forest. They seemed to always be near, as if they were drawn to her the way that she was drawn to the village children. Since she was kind to them, sharing with them whatever food and shelter she found, they liked her. But their companionship was not enough, not nearly enough to stop the loneliness that was rising in the girl as she grew.

None of the villagers would tolerate her. When she was very young, there were small kindnesses here and there, but as her company of animals increased as she grew older, she was seen as something suspicious, something not right, something to be shunned. People would throw things at her to shoo her away, crying out *devochka yaga* (horrible girl), and then cross themselves in case there was evil with her. Village children were told stories by the adults to warn them away from her. There was one man, however, who did not fear her. He seemed a gruff and unpredictable sort. He was not from the village but from much farther away and had a thick Russian accent. Though he rarely spoke to her, he would seek her out and leave her things. She only saw him once or twice a season. Even though he left her helpful things, like shoes, blankets, and pots, she didn't like him and wished he would stop coming. She didn't even know his name.

As our story begins, the girl with no name had decided that today was the day she would make a friend. It was a beautiful spring day, the kind that lifts a person's heart and makes them feel like anything is possible. She had brought along her prettiest birds, who were now perched on the pine branches all around her. Sunlight sprinkled through the tree branches and dappled the roof of the small dwelling. This hut was the place that Rechenka lived, who was the girl she liked the best. So she enjoyed the spring breeze and the twittering of the birds around her and dozed a little as she waited for Rechenka to finish her indoor chores and come outside.

Suddenly, several children burst out of the house, banging the door behind them, running straight for the path on the edge of the yard that led into the village. They pushed and yelled dares at each other. These were boys, noisy and unlikable, and she had no use for them. She turned from them to look at the open doorway and saw the children's mother step out of the house, red in the face and out of breath from whatever chore she had been doing. She yelled an exasperated reminder to the boys about something to get in the village, but she knew the boys had not heard her. She stood there for a moment, moving some stray hair from her face, taking a momentary respite from the endless work that awaited her return. It was then that Rechenka appeared at the open doorway. The girl with no name became fully awake and looked at Rechenka hungrily. She didn't know exactly how, or if, her plan would work, but she had high hopes, the kind of blind hope that only a child can have.

Rechenka's mother turned and saw her daughter in the doorway. She picked up a basket from the grass and pointed at the chickens across the yard, setting her at the task of collecting eggs. Though her voice was a bit sharp, she tousled Rechenka's hair as she moved past her and back into the hut. The door to the hut remained open as Rechenka made her way slowly across the yard, past the chickens who were busily pecking at bugs in the grass, to the edge of the trees. It was time. The girl with no name whispered to the smallest, daintiest bird, and it flitted across the yard, landing a little ways away from Rechenka. Rechenka was delighted to see a bird so close and took a small step towards it, then more when the bird didn't fly away. Everytime she got very close, the bird hopped a little farther away, but staying close enough that the girl wouldn't lose hope. In this way, the little bird worked the girl across the yard and to the edge of the pine trees. The girl with no name watched as Rechenka hesitated on the edge, wanting to touch the little bird but knowing better than to step into the dimly lit forest alone. It was time for the girl with no name to make her move.

"Hello, Rechenka," she said. Rechenka looked around with both fear and curiosity; it took only moments for curiosity to get the better of her.

"Who is there? How do you know my name?" The girl with no name wasn't sure how to answer. She stepped closer so Rechenka could see her. Rechenka took a step backwards and said, "Oh, aren't you the *devochka yaga* that everyone chases away?"

"No," she quickly lied. Then she thought better of it and said, "I am the *devochka* that gets chased away, but I'm not *yaga*." She held her breath and tried to look friendly. She really wanted this to go well. "What does *yaga* mean, anyway?"

"*Yaga* means a horrible thing, something that might be dangerous," said Rechenka.

The girl thought a moment and replied, "I'm not dangerous." She didn't say she might be dangerous, because she had observed over the years that some of the things she did were not things the villagers were able to do. She had never seen them talking to animals with understanding, and she had never seen them start fires or create springs of fresh water from the ground just by wishing for it. But some of the things she could do…sometimes she scared herself.

Rechenka had taken a few steps into the trees and could now see all the birds on the branches around the girl. "Oooh, those are pretty! Why do they stay so near to you, *yaga*? Do you think one would let me hold it?"

"Would you like to hold one even if I was *yaga*?" the girl with no name asked; meanwhile, she had already begun to think of this as a name for herself.

Rechenka considered this as she reached a hand out for a bird. "You seem nice to me." At this, Yaga whispered to the bird, and it hopped onto the girl's hand for just a moment, then back onto the tree branch.

"We are too close to your hut, the birds are nervous here. Can you come a little further into the forest?" Rechenka thought about this and looked doubtfully over her shoulder at the chickens and her hut.

"We wouldn't have to go far for them to like you more," Yaga said tantalizingly.

"Well, all right, but I can't be gone too long or my mother will miss me." Rechenka said this in a matter-of-fact tone, but the words ignited a flame of jealousy in Yaga's heart. Rechenka didn't see the brief, dark look pass over Yaga's face since she was absorbed with the birds.

"Come." And the *devochka yaga* led the pretty girl deeper into the woods, farther away from her home. And the pretty girl was never seen again.

Over the course of the next few years, many young girls went missing. On five separate occasions other children had spotted Yaga nearby on those days, for it was harder for her to hide as she grew up. Fear grew in the village as family after family would lose a beloved daughter, and the villagers feared the worst. They sent out groups of men to scour the forest, hoping to find the girls or at least a trace of them, to no avail. Stories and rumors sprung up over the years that laid the blame on Yaga, and parents started to warn their children not to stray away alone or to ever talk to the ugly girl lest she lure them away and feed them to an ogre, or perhaps eat them for breakfast herself. But one by one, Yaga still tried to catch someone who would be her friend. It never worked out, and in her disappointment she would turn them into a small tree or a flowering bush. In this way, even though they had rejected her, they would always have to stay in the forest with her and would never leave. It made her only a little less lonely to sit beside what had once been a girl and talk to them like how she imagined friends talked to each other, but only a little for the tree or the bush could never reply.

As Yaga was turning into a young woman, her desire for a companion grew. She traveled farther and wider, looking for someone to finally be her friend. The number of once-humans in the forest continued to grow, some of them boys and young men that had bothered her one way or another, or sometimes just because they were there and she could. Yaga didn't like boys, so they would be turned into rotten tree stumps full of worms. A worse fate awaited any men who came looking to find the lost girls or to test their mettle against her, and their bones piled up in a deep recess of the mountains. The gruff man who was not from the village would come and visit more frequently, riding in on his big, beautiful *bogatyr* horse. He seemed to be interested in how she did her magic. He was especially interested to hear about how she turned people into plants or other things. He stayed one time for a week just to watch her do it. He seemed almost proud, and when Yaga asked him why, he told her that he was her father. Father! Yaga was stunned to hear this, and then she turned very angry.

"If you are my father, why did you never take me to live in your home? Why did you never tell me?" Yaga's heart felt as though it would burst at the anger mixed with happiness inside her. She had a family at last!

"I don't have a home, *devochka duratskiy* (stupid girl). I am far too busy to have a home. And why did you need to know that when you were younger, you just would have wanted to come with me when you were perfectly fine here and had everything you needed," the man said in a very uncaring tone.

Any happiness in her heart faded away, and Yaga spluttered for a moment in her anger before she could form words. "Everything I needed? Everything I needed? I have been cold and hungry and lonely every year that I can remember! Everything I needed! How about a home and a bed and warm food?" In the midst of her tirade a quiet thought, full of hope, appeared in her mind. "And where is my mother, then?!"

The man replied immediately. "She is dead." Without further comment, he whistled to his *bogatyr* horse, swung himself up onto the mighty stallion, and was gone, leaving Yaga standing alone. Yaga ran and ran until she could run no longer, and slept that night on the forest floor where she had fallen.

After that, Yaga did nothing at all. She grew bitter about what she had never had, the sense of it sharper now that she knew her father had known her whereabouts the whole time and still she had grown up a vagabond in the forest. She would have surely starved or died of thirst had not her animal friends cared for her, leaving food and water for her and staying with her in this low time. Twice her father came but only observed her from afar. Yaga sensed him but had no energy to even look up. The third time he came, many weeks later, it was clear that, despite the animals' efforts, Yaga was truly weak and things did not look good. Not wanting to lose his only offspring, especially since she had a magic ability like her mother, he tried to fix things.

"Yaga, daughter, what is making you like this? Are you not glad to learn that you have a father?"

Yaga stirred herself and lifted her eyes from the ground a little. "I have grown up so lonely in this place, scavenging for food, when I had a father who could have taken care of me," she said in a sad voice.

"I can be a father to no one. Don't you know who I am? Haven't you heard the villagers talk of me?" Here he paused for her answer. When none came, he said, "I am Koshchei the Deathless, and I have far more important things to do than to take care of a child."

This finally got Yaga to lift her eyes up to his. She repeated, "Koshchei the Deathless? The ogre that whisks away young women and is feared by everyone?"

"I am the one and the same. So you see why I only visited and made sure you were surviving all right. Your mother, though, loved you very much even before you were born, and she died trying to save you and herself—from me."

Yaga's face finally seemed to come to life again as she said to Koshchei, "Tell me everything about my mother."

"Your mother was a young woman I had stolen from some village far on the other side of the mountains and then farther still. I usually have one to keep me company until I tire of her, and then...well, then that one dies and I just get another. I could tell your mother was different soon after she arrived in my lands. I didn't know why she seemed so calm and accepting of her plight until I realized she must have a special ability and be biding her time. I would disguise myself as a bird and keep an eye on her. Sure enough, she was a *yaga*, she had the power of magic inside herself. Katya, yes, Katya was her name. She used the magic to do her chores, and I knew it would only be a matter of time until she used it to try to escape from or harm me. But of all the girls that I had taken, your mother was the most pleasing to me, and I kept her the longest, possibly several years, who can remember? I might have kept her a very long time if she hadn't run away. It took me months to track her down—I believe she changed herself into different animals as she traveled, and she stayed one step ahead of me for a long time. I found that I missed her, but more than that I wanted to have her magic at my disposal. I have many powers, but the more power the better, eh? When I finally came upon her, she was in human form and was holding a baby. It was clear that she was dying. She asked me to send her baby back to the village she had come from, then whispered some things and held her hands over the baby. They glowed, and then the baby glowed. I have seen enough in my long life to know that she had just transferred her magic to you, though it is usually with a much older child that this is done. But your mother had no choice, she was dying. Her final words were a warning, "If you do not send my baby to my village, if you keep her, it will be your undoing in the end." And then she died. And of course I have kept you since you are mine now and your magic is mine now, too. You are old enough now to come with me and to use your magic to help me do what I want." Finally Koshchei ended his tale.

Yaga sat still for a long time thinking about what Koshchei had said. Finally she said, "So my mother escaped you by changing herself into something else?" And with that, Yaga closed her eyes and dissolved into a wisp of fog and floated away from Koshchei and from all the things she now knew.

Yaga existed like this and that, most of the time just as drifting leaves or a bird or a breeze, for quite some time. She hoped her father would never be able to find her again. After several years had passed, she found herself in another land, near a village far on the other side of the mountains and then farther still. No one here knew her, and she could walk among the villagers as a young woman who was a bit unkempt and more than a little wild looking. People assumed she was from some settlement farther away, and though they were not friendly, at least they didn't drive her away. Yaga asked a few people selling things in a market if they had heard of a Katya. No one would answer her until finally one of the older women clucked and said, "Oh, Katya, that is a name I haven't heard spoken for years and years. Why do you ask about Katya, young one?" The woman took a more careful look at her, taking in her ragged clothes and unkempt hair.

Yaga didn't know what to say, so she simply told the truth. "She was my mother, and I wanted to see where she was from." Yaga remained standing before the woman, almost holding her breath in hopes of an answer.

"You are her daughter? How can this be? She was seen being dragged away by Koshchei the Deathless, that villain, and no girl taken by him has ever gotten free." The old woman sat up a little straighter on the bench beside the woven fabrics she was selling.

Yaga looked around at all the other merchants and villagers nearby and hesitated. She had a good feeling about this old woman, but it didn't seem like the right place to explain her story. The old woman realized the problem when Yaga just kept looking around without replying.

"Ah, young one, you are wise. Tales are best told beside the hearth, not on the open street. Come home with me, I will give you a bite to eat and listen to your story about Katya, for I was a good friend of her mother's, and Katya was very dear to me. But tell me, is there any hope that she still lives?" Yaga felt bad about the hope sparkling in the old woman's eyes.

"No, she is dead. I was a baby when it happened," said Yaga with little emotion, for she never knew her mother.

"Aaagh, well, I knew it was this way in my heart, for it was many years ago that I did my grieving for your mother. Come, child, help me pack up my wares and we will head to my home." After a pause, she added, "you may call me *babushka*, since I am old enough—and then some—to be your grandmother." Yaga and the old woman packed everything into a cart, and together they pushed it through the village and a little ways into the forest. A small stone hut, hidden in the shade of the trees and partially covered with ivy, came into view, and it was into this hut that the woman took Yaga.

"Sit down, sit down, I will wake the fire and we will have some tea." Yaga didn't have any manners, so instead of offering to help, she sat down in front of the large *pech* (oven) while Babushka slowly set some tea and biscuits on a plate for Yaga. "Tell me, young one, before we begin the story, what is your name?" she asked as she handed Yaga the plate.

Yaga was so hungry that she ripped off a big bite and hastily gulped some tea before answering, "Yaga."

Babushka looked alarmed, but only for a moment. "Now I remember, Katya had gifts of which we knew very little, for most people with gifts try to keep them hidden lest they be driven out. It would make sense that her daughter would inherit some of her gifts. But who would name a young girl *yaga*?"

"Why? What does it mean?"

"Well, to our people it means a witch, someone who can command the creatures and control the very space around them. But it also can mean something bad, something horrible, something to be feared."

"It is what the villagers near where I lived called me when they chased me away." Here Yaga paused to eat more biscuit and drink more tea, using no manners whatsoever since she had never been taught those things.

"You are a wild child, aren't you, poor thing. If your mother is dead, what of your father? Who raised you?"

Yaga hesitated, fearing that as soon as it was known that Koshchei was her father she would be made to leave. But she found herself wanting to tell this woman everything, and so she did. She started with Koshchei's tale of her mother and then told of her own growing up in the woods. Babushka's face grew angry during the part about Yaga turning all those girls into part of the forest, but by the time Yaga had finished she had regained her composure.

Talking almost more to herself than to Yaga, Babushka clucked her tongue, saying, "Well, what can you expect to be happening with no mother and with that devil Koshchei for a father. Yaga, you must not do that to anyone again."

Yaga stayed with Babushka as days turned into weeks, and weeks into months. She wandered the nearby forests in the company of small creatures during the day while Babushka went about her business in the village, but the two spent the evenings together, cozy by the *pech* and safe from the cold, snowy winds outside. Babushka enjoyed teaching Yaga about many things, about family and village manners and the history of the people of the area. But the thing Yaga liked to hear about the most were the stories that Babushka told. There were stories of Finist the Bright Falcon, of the tsar's son, Prince Ivan, of *rusalkis* lurking in the streams, waiting to ensnare handsome young men, of the goddess Mokosh and Saint Paraskeva who waited to punish any girl or woman who dares to spin and weave on Fridays, and many other tales about heroes accomplishing great things through determination and with the help of magic. She especially wanted to hear any story relating to her father, Koshchei. Thanks to Babushka, she now knew why he was called deathless. But Yaga now knew that he was not truly deathless after hearing the prescribed way to bring about his end, if the stories were true. But there was never any explanation about how he came to be evil, why he did the cruel and heartless things he did.

Spring came, and with it a renewed sense of hope in Yaga that she might yet get what she wanted. Knowing she had stayed with Babushka far too long, and also knowing that Koshchei was always keeping tabs on her, she said goodbye to Babushka. Babushka was sad to see this wild young woman go, but at least she had taught her a bit more understanding about people. Hopefully Yaga would have a better sense of right and wrong. Yaga was sad to leave this homey, friendly hut, and she would miss the caring and kindness of this older woman. But go she must, and after many weeks of travel, going slowly enough for her forest creatures to accompany her, and after going far on the other side of the mountains and then farther still, she arrived back in her own forest.

She wasted no time in putting the plan that she had formed during her stay at Babushka's house into action. First, she created a hut of her own. She used magic to make it, and it turned out a bit unusual. When she spoke aloud her desire for a hut that would not be seen by foes, her magic created a hut on legs—chicken legs, to be exact—that could move itself further into the forest to avoid being noticed. And her desire for a secure hut that not just anyone could walk into was interpreted by the magic that the door would always face away from an unfriendly guest unless they knew the words to request that the hut turn around and have the door face them. Yaga had enjoyed sitting before Babushka's *pech* so much, especially in the winter weather, that she created an extra-large *pech* for her own hut's kitchen.

At last the hut was finished. Yaga felt more settled than she ever had, now with a home of her own. She tamed the forest around the hut, just slightly, creating a somewhat wild yard full of flowers, herbs, and vegetables. To separate it from the forest, she built a fence made from the bones she had hidden on the mountain ages and ages ago, a warning to anyone who would come poking around. The last ingredient to complete the home she was making for herself was a baby. A baby would not disappoint Yaga like every single girl had, and Yaga started planning how to best get one. She knew that she could never have a husband, for she had no tolerance for boys and men. And she needed a husband, or at least some man, to have her own baby. And then there was the problem of what if she had a baby boy. It all seemed so much less problematic to just steal a baby girl. Even though Yaga now had a rudimentary sense of right and wrong from her talks with Babushka, her wild formative years and the influence of such a villainous father won out. And so Yaga set off to find a baby.

The first baby lived a week and a half. The second baby she stole died quickly also. Yaga didn't know what she was doing wrong, but she was lacking some essential knowledge about babies. The third time she stole an older baby, but it just kept happening. The yard beside her hut on chicken legs became slowly dotted with more and more tiny graves. Yaga planted roses around them, and the yard took on a sad beauty. Stories of babies being whisked away by the *devochka yaga* all grown up spread far and wide, and everyone feared for their babies, creating charms and rituals to keep Yaga away. Men sent looking for the missing babies never returned, and her pile of bones in the mountain grew higher. Finally, Yaga's broken sense of right and wrong worked well enough for her to see that these things were exactly what Babushka had told her never to do again, and so she put an end to it and accepted her loneliness.

Years slowly passed, season after season that saw Yaga growing into a woman and then into someone older still. Her wild, tangled hair was now mostly a dull gray that hung below her knees, and her already rough looks had been tarnished further by the loneliness and bitterness of the passing years. Her large nose looked even larger against her cheeks sunken with age, and her hours spent working on her magic had given her shoulders a pronounced stoop. The creatures of the forest still gathered around her, and some had taken up residence in her yard, even inside the hut itself. And this is how Yaga existed for many years, using magic and forest knowledge to keep herself out of sight from people who wished her harm. This meant from all people, for everyone in the countryside far and wide had heard and believed the stories of the terrible *baba yaga* (horrible woman), as she was now known due to her mature years. It had been years and years since Baba Yaga had last seen her father, that evil Koshchei, and she was thankful for that. But that did not mean that he had not been using other means of spying on her and keeping track of Baba Yaga's magic abilities, and he now knew quite a lot about her powers and how she used them.

On an unremarkable day in late fall, when the leaves had already fallen and become a carpet of crisp brown on the forest floor, a girl came wandering along in the forest. Baba Yaga's forest creatures hurried to tell her about the girl, and just as she felt her hut stir as it started its motions to turn and to move further into the dense trees, something made Baba Yaga pause and watch. The girl walked slowly, with her head down and her feet dragging. Though she was rather small, her shape told that she was becoming a young woman. Tangled waves of dark hair framed her face, and what a face it was! It seemed the most beautiful face that Baba Yaga had ever seen. Baba Yaga stood motionless inside her hut, intently watching this girl's slow approach. Something about this girl had stirred something buried deep within Baba Yaga for years, but it had been so long that she no longer knew what the feeling meant.

The hut turned slowly and silently to hide its door, for this function of the hut was something that Baba Yaga could not change. Baba Yaga crossed the hut's interior to keep watching the girl. Would she notice the hut? Would she approach? Would she know what to ask for? And if all these things happened successfully, would Baba Yaga be her eventual demise?

The girl almost trudged past without seeing the hut, but after she had already passed the yard and was headed further on, a crow that resided in one of Baba Yaga's trees emitted a loud, harsh squawk.

This noise stopped the girl, and she looked up and noticed the primitive-looking hut set well back from the path she was taking. Now that her face was more easily seen, Baba Yaga could see the thinness of it, the pinched look of hunger that mixed itself with the beauty of the girl's face. Baba Yaga remembered that feeling of hunger from when she herself was a girl, existing on scraps and what she could forage in the forest. She found herself both hoping and fearing that the girl would know what to say to the hut so she could gain entrance.

The girl stood still for a long time, wistfully looking at the hut as the cold wind blew around her worn clothes and tangled hair. She seemed to be thinking of other things, other places, maybe. Baba Yaga couldn't stop the hope in her heart from spilling out as magic, and in that moment snow began to fall, first as a few flakes, then as swirling curtains. The snow seemed to snap the girl out of her reverie, and she pulled her old coat tighter and walked toward the hut. She opened the gate, her hand recoiling when she realized the gate and the fence were made from bones and not wood. But the driving snow pushed her into the yard and up to the wall of the hut. The girl peered through the snow, searching for a door that wasn't there. She then pleaded, "Hut, turn your back to the forest and your face toward me." The moment the words were spoken, the hut turned around, and the steps that led up to the front porch and the thick wooden door were right before her feet. She climbed them carefully and walked across the creaking wood of the porch to stand at the door. Barely had she touched the great iron ring on the door when it swung open into the dimly lit interior. A last gust of snowy wind pushed her inside, and the door shut itself behind her with a loud thud. Outside, the snow vanished as if it had never been there at all.

The beautiful girl looked around the room she found herself in but couldn't see much, not even Baba Yaga standing by one of the windows. Flickering light from the fire in the *pech* tempted the girl to cross the dark part of the room and enter the kitchen area. She immediately crouched down near the fire to warm herself, pulling off her rag mittens and holding her hands out to the flames.

"Are you fleeing a deed or doing a deed?" queried Baba Yaga in her scratchy voice from the dark part of the hut. The girl was too cold and hungry to jump up quickly, but she turned toward the voice with great fear on her face.

"Oh! I'm sorry to enter your hut, but I was so cold. Please forgive me," the girl said quickly.

"But you didn't answer my question. Are you fleeing a deed or doing a deed?" Baba Yaga repeated, more slowly this time.

The girl thought a moment, though it was hard to think through her fear and hunger and cold, and finally replied, "I am doing both, I think." A log in the fire popped loudly, and the girl tried to jump up this time. She ended up slumping down even further in her weak state and pleaded, "Please, I beg you for shelter for the night, and perhaps a bite of food. Your kindness will be repaid…" And with this she lost consciousness and lay motionless on the floor in front of the *pech*.

Baba Yaga moved into the light of the kitchen area and looked down at the sleeping young woman. She stayed still a long time, just watching her lie there. At last Baba Yaga undid the clasp of her thick cloak and laid it across the girl with surprising gentleness. She settled into a chair at the rough wooden table and began a silent vigil that would last the entire night, giving her hours and hours to think about her past and the things she had done.

After the passing of that night and most of the next day, the girl woke up. She was alone, for Baba Yaga had gone out for the day to attend to some tasks. A bowl of soup was sitting on the *pech*, and a small loaf of bread sat on the table alongside a spoon and a cup of cool, clear water. The girl tentatively asked hello twice, then ate and drank every morsel that had been left for her. She was sitting there at the table, wishing she had more to eat and drink, when the door of the hut opened and in walked Baba Yaga, carrying a basket of various roots and berries.

"Oh ho, *devochka*, I see you have awakened and eaten what was left for you," Baba Yaga declared in her scratchy voice as she approached the table.

The girl had the kindest of hearts, but even so it was hard for her not to show disgust at the sight of the approaching old woman. The sunken face, the huge nose, the wild, tangled hair were alarming, indeed. The girl chose to be brave and replied, "Yes, thank you, *baba dobryy* (kind woman), you have saved my life, and I don't know how I can repay you."

"Tsk, tsk, that is easy. Tell me who you are and why you are out so far in the forest at such a time of year, and I will know what to ask of you."

The girl pulled Baba Yaga's cloak around her more tightly and started her story from the beginning. Her name was Mariska, and she was from a faraway village. Her parents had been weavers until her mother died a few years ago. Her father remarried, and this woman had a daughter near the age of Mariska, though that girl was very plain-looking and mean to boot. The stepmother became jealous of the attention that Mariska received because of her beauty and her kind nature and swore to extinguish the light that was making her own daughter look bad. At first it had just been confining Mariska to the home and giving her more chores to do, but then tasks that snagged her hair, ripped her clothes, and dirtied her appearance were added, soon to be followed by more dangerous tasks. The father, though he loved his own daughter, was busy with work and wanted to keep his new wife happy. So no one came to the aid of Mariska. One day, several weeks ago, as late fall prepared to turn into winter, she had heard her stepmother and stepsister plotting to end her life. The stepmother planned to send Mariska out to visit a distant relative of the stepmother's. No such relative existed, and the stepmother's directions were intended to lose Mariska in the wilderness, hopefully never to be seen again. Mariska had no choice but to set out on this doomed journey. She wandered for several weeks, able to beg or to find a bit of something to eat every few days, and she had been on her very last leg when she walked past Baba Yaga's hut.

"So, you see, *baba dobryy*, I am both fleeing my stepmother and also trying to find a place to stay." Mariska ended her story with a sigh.

The girl's story had stirred something deep within Baba Yaga, but she tried to push it back down because it made her feel uncomfortable. But she did extend charity to the girl by saying, "You are welcome to stay in my little house for the present, for you sound as alone as I am." Her voice was gruff and scratchy, but Mariska could hear the underlying kindness in the message.

"Thank you, *baba dobryy*! And what should I call you?"

Baba Yaga was loathe to turn this girl against her so soon by revealing her name that was so hated and feared, so she decided not to say it. "What's in a name? You may call me *babushka* for now," she told the girl, thinking of what the old woman in her mother's village had told Baba Yaga so many years ago.

And so Mariska was kept busy in the days to come with various tasks and tests put to her by Baba Yaga as she prepared the yard and the hut for the arrival of winter, giving Baba Yaga more time to wander the forest to forage for food and to practice her magic. Some tasks she left for Mariska were tricky or seemed impossible, like filling a bath for Baba Yaga's hut creatures using a sieve to transport the water or dusting the inside of the hut with nothing but a bare stick. In these instances, because she was never anything but kind with them, the small birds and creatures that lived in the hut and in the yard spoke to Mariska and gave her the knowledge or the materials to fulfill the tasks. Her unwavering kindness and pure goodness could be felt by the animals. The songbirds instructed Marsika how to use the thick clay to coat the interior of the sieve so that it could carry water, and the gray cat that slept up in the loft gathered feathers from the crows outside for her to use to fashion a feather duster from the bare stick. Baba Yaga was gruff and seemed neither impressed nor surprised when the girl completed each task, no matter how tricky, but inside the feeling she had when first seeing the girl began to grow, starting to warm Baba Yaga's soul and thaw her heart.

Marsika continued to stay all during the long winter, as there was plenty of food and Baba Yaga never said anything about her having to leave. She kept herself busy during the short days by spinning thread and weaving cloth at the large loom that Baba Yaga had built. It took up much of one side of the hut. Though the girl did not realize it, the loom was constructed with magic, so the cloth that was produced was the finest quality no matter the skill of the weaver. Baba Yaga began to realize that Mariska might be able to take the cloth to the market in the spring, something that Baba Yaga could never do. Evenings were spent in front of the *pech*, with Mariska telling Baba Yaga many new stories that she had never heard from the long-ago woman in her mother's village and with Baba Yaga making up new ones to enthrall the girl. Baba Yaga was content; she was happy for the first time in her life, though she did not realize what the feeling was. She wondered if the girl would want to leave her in the spring, and if she did, Baba Yaga wondered if she would be able to let her go, or would the girl become a beautiful climbing rose in the wild yard? Baba Yaga had become quite fond of this girl despite trying not to, and she hoped she would be able to stop herself from turning Mariska into a climbing rose if she was thrown into the depths of disappointment by her departure. She just didn't know.

Sometimes Mariska would look sad, and Baba Yaga would ask what was troubling her. Mariska, who had grown to love Baba Yaga almost as if she were her real babushka, did not want to hurt her feelings by talking about the mother she missed so terribly. She would just sigh and say, "It seems silly to miss something that is no longer there, but sometimes I cannot help but think about my happy childhood days before everything changed." And Mariska, being the good girl she truly was, would add, "But it has turned out better than

I would have ever imagined, for I never expected to find a snug home with a *babushka* just for me." At this, Baba Yaga would abruptly change the conversation, for she was not used to anyone liking her.

Finally, the days started to lengthen and signs of spring began to appear in the forest. Mariska frequently bathed Baba Yaga's animals, who were forever getting muddy at this time of year, without being asked. She was so gentle with each one that they sometimes got muddy on purpose to enjoy her attentions. Baba Yaga herself let Mariska clean her up a bit. Mariska carefully picked out tangles and debris from Baba Yaga's hair, cut it a bit shorter—above her waist, and washed and brushed it. Looking better, and feeling better, Baba Yaga began to stand a little straighter. Her clothes, washed and mended properly by Mariska, without being asked, made her look even nicer still. Though Mariska had begun to love Baba Yaga even when she looked her worst, she found it easier to pretend that Baba Yaga was her real, true babushka.

One particularly lovely day, Mariska asked, "Babushka, would you allow me to have a small space in the yard for some flowers and plants of my own?"

Baba Yaga stood still, her back to Mariska as she sorted some herbs for casting spells on the table. What kind of a question was this? Did this mean that Mariska intended to stay? Or was she to be yet even more cruelly disappointed? Today was the day to find out, one way or another.

"*Devochka*, won't you be leaving here soon to go back to your people?" she asked in a throaty voice.

"Babushka, I have told you that I no longer have a family or a home," the girl reminded her. "I have nowhere else to go, but if you want me to leave, I will do so," she said in a sad voice.

"So you want to stay here, living with such an old *baba* as me?" Baba Yaga asked, her back still turned to the girl. "I have never told you my name. Surely you have heard stories about me, terrible stories told by the people throughout the land. You should know that I am

Ba—"

"Stop!" Mariska cried out. "I can guess what your real name is, but don't say it to me, please. You have always been fair and good to me, and I have passed all of the tricky tests and tasks you have set before me, and all is well between us. To me you are the *babushka* that I have never had, and that is who you shall stay."

Baba Yaga turned around, and for the first time in her life there was a tear in her eye. "*Devochka*, you are now my *vnuchka* (granddaughter) and can stay here with me for always." And the two women, one young and one old, embraced with great happiness and love.

Spring turned into summer, and all was going well for Baba Yaga and Mariska until a cold dark day took hold in September. Baba Yaga had a bad feeling about the cold wind and warned Mariska to stay in the yard as she left to collect special flower seeds on the mountain for her magic. But it wasn't good enough, for the cold wind was Koshchei. He had tired of everything else in this world and had come to check on his daughter and her magic. Over the years he had sent people that he had transformed into animals to spy on her and her magic deeds, so he knew quite a lot about her ways and her magic. But she was getting old now, and he was done waiting. This time he would make her talk to him, to share her magic with him whether she wanted to or not, and then he would be even more powerful. He planned to tempt her with the secret of how to become deathless; at her age, that should be very tempting indeed.

Koshchei cantered up to the bone fence on his great *bogatyr* horse. The horse was both powerful and beautiful, with rippling muscles and barely restrained power under his sable coat, and his speed was often the reason Koshchei got away after one of his evil deeds.

"Yaga, daughter of mine, I have come to see you. Come and greet your father," Koshchei yelled at the hut. But the hut remained silent, showing only its back to him. The yard, too, was deserted of animals, for the unsettling wind and Baba Yaga's warning to Mariska had sent them for shelter.

"I know your secrets. You can't keep me out, you *baba duratskiy* (stupid woman)." And with that, Koshchei stepped back and commanded the hut, "Turn your back to the forest, and your front to me," just as his spies had told him to say. The hut on chicken legs rotated and stopped with the front door across the bone fence from Koshchei. "At last," he said eagerly as he opened the bony gate, climbed the steps, and let himself into the hut.

Mariska had planned to obey Baba Yaga's warning, but the animals had told her of a crow with a broken wing from this evil weather. Mariska had searched a little ways into the forest beyond the yard until she found the poor crow, who was very upset at his inability to fly. Mariska examined the broken wing and realized it needed to be fixed inside the hut with the supplies there. She was carrying the crow carefully across the yard toward the hut when the crow suddenly lurched out of her arms to the ground, cawing a warning.

"Crow, I have fixed many bird wings, and everything will be fine if you go into the house with me," Mariska said reassuringly. Her assurance fell on deaf ears, and the crow continued to squawk and hop away from the hut. The wind fell for a brief moment, and in that moment the bird whispered, "Koshchei!" before hopping awkwardly away.

A terrible feeling came over Mariska, a sense of doom like none she had ever felt. She was afraid to turn around, but she was equally terrified to continue standing with her back to the hut. She willed her legs to turn her around, and the hut came into view. Standing at the window was a tall, evil-looking man, staring at her with a hungry look. Mariska was frozen with fear.

Koshchei, who had quickly gone through the hut and the loft looking for Baba Yaga, had spotted the girl walking through the yard. At first he had dismissed her since she was a young girl, and his mind was focused on finding the old woman Baba Yaga. But then he had caught a glimpse of her face. Her face! It was mesmerizing in its beauty. Indeed, Koshchei had not seen a face like this in his entire evil life. The young women he took for his own over the years had always been the prettiest in their villages, but this, this took his breath away, and he immediately became obsessed with having this beauty. What she was doing in his daughter's yard, he didn't know, but she seemed at home and not the least bit frightened. It only took a moment for the scene to change, and as the crow she had been carrying escaped toward the forest, fear seemed to come over the girl's body. She began to shake as she stood there, then slowly turned to face the hut, to face the window where he stood. When their eyes met, he spoke certain words under his breath to mark her as his, and his words flew on the wind to the four corners of the earth as he exited the hut. He strode toward the still frozen girl, threw her over his shoulder roughly, and carried her to his *bogatyr* horse which stood waiting on the other side of the bony gate. He tossed her across its back, mounted behind her, and rode away, triumphant in his capture of the most beautiful creature he had ever seen. Mariska, frozen in Koshchei's trance, could make no move of her own, and the only expression of her horror and sorrow at being taken away by Koshchei was a single tear that ran down her cheek and fell onto the forest path as the hut faded from her view. And then she was gone.

Baba Yaga knew right away that something terrible had happened when she returned from her ingredient gathering. Her hut came into view, but the front door was facing her and swinging ajar, a dark hole into an empty hut.

"Mariska, *vnuchka*, are you in the yard?" As Baba Yaga drew closer to the bony gate, something glittery on the path in front of her caught her eye. It was Mariska's tear. She leaned over to catch the tear on her finger, then lifted it to her mouth and tasted it. It was full of the sadness and horror that Mariska had felt the moment she made the tear, and it confirmed Baba Yaga's suspicions that something terrible had occurred. She ran into the hut, and immediately the

Russian scent hit her large nose.

"I smell the Russian scent, and even stronger, the smell of evil," Baba Yaga announced to the empty hut. A sudden realization came over her, and an anger rose up in her like never before, a deadly anger.

"Koshchei! You will pay for this with your life," she vowed. Wasting no time, she started to pack all the supplies and magic items she would need for her quest to save her beloved *vnuchka* and to put an end to the evil Koshchei. It had been many years since Baba Yaga had used her flying mortar—not since her baby stealing days, in fact, but now the time had come to bring it out, along with the pestle to steer with and the broom to erase her tracks.

Months passed, late summer turned into fall, then fall into winter, and still Baba Yaga had not discovered where Koshchei had taken Mariska. Her animal friends had scattered across the land to help her gather information, and many of the ones that had been over the mountains and then farther still reported back that several of those distant villages had been visited by Koshchei since early fall, but that Koshchei had been alone every time. Baba Yaga knew that Koshchei could travel great distances with his fine *bogatyr* horse. But she also knew that he would not want to stray too far or too long from a new young woman in his possession, especially not one so beautiful as Mariska, so she pointed her mortar to head north, over the mountains and then farther still.

In her mortar, Baba Yaga searched endless miles of empty forests for the remainder of winter, using magic to keep warm and her woodland creatures to help her find food as she searched. She focused on the search and on what magic she could use to get rid of Koshchei; she tried not to let her mind stray to thoughts of Mariska and what she must be enduring, it was too much. Her resolve strengthened by the day as she tirelessly searched.

All this time, Mariska had been Koshchei's captive, living in a large underground area he had built to house the young women he stole. It was in terrible condition, dirty and ramshackle, and at first Mariska worked each day to make the place decent. Dust and cobwebs covered everything since it had been so long since Koshchei had kidnapped anyone. In some areas there were heaps of bones, some from animals and some most decidedly not, and Mariska tried to ignore them and what they foreshadowed. Thankfully, in the beginning Koshchei was not around most of the time. When he was there, he mostly sat and watched her, or stood close to her, all of which was unsettling. He occasionally led her to different rooms of the place and seemed to be on the verge of making a decision of some sort, but then he would abruptly leave. Finally, one day he didn't leave, and Mariska found out what his mind had been dwelling on all those weeks. Her situation was truly the most desperate it could be now, but escape from her underground prison seemed to be impossible.

Winter arrived and dragged on for months, and during all this time of Koshchei's more and more frequent visits, Mariska started to give up any hope of anything. Not an hour passed that she did not shed tears for her little hut and her *babushka*. She realized that her future was to become a small pile of bones in this prison like all the young women who had been here before her, and with each passing day she began to wish for it to come soon. Well, not all the young women had become piles of bones, for she remembered one of the stories that her *babushka* had told her of a girl named Katya who had escaped the evil Koshchei using magic. But, sighed Mariska, she had no magic, and the things that she did have, her goodness and her beauty, were both being eroded away with every visit from Koshchei.

Mariska hoped that her desolate state would make Koshchei lose interest in her and just let her die, but Koshchei, that devil, found something even more attractive about her broken state, about the change he was making to her beauty. Not destroying it, but rather making it even more appealing to him in a tarnished state, like a ray of sun seen through a stained glass window once beautiful but now in disrepair, the beauty of both the sun and the glass still visible through the dirt and the cracks.

Koshchei was expecting Baba Yaga to find the girl eventually, once he realized that Mariska and Baba Yaga were like *vnuchka* and *babushka* to each other. If she came when the girl was still alive, he would use the girl as a bargaining chip for Baba Yaga's magic. If not, well, then, Koshchei wasn't worried. He was an arrogant son of a bitch and was sure he could get what he wanted from Baba Yaga one way or another.

Baba Yaga forged on through the winter weather, searching and searching. She needed to find Mariska before it was too late, before her father had enough time to first destroy and then to kill Mariska. Finally, one day she caught a Russian scent near a jumble of boulders in a hilly area. She hid her mortar in a nearby thicket and approached the rocky pile, erasing her tracks in the snow with her broom. A steady stream of warmer air touched her face as she investigated the spaces in between the huge rocks. The Russian scent became stronger still, and on the other side of the rocks there were large horse tracks in the snow mixed with boot tracks, and Baba Yaga knew that this was one of Koshchei's haunts. But was he there now? Was this where her Mariska was imprisoned? Baba Yaga forced herself to retreat a short distance to some trees. She concealed herself with magic and sat down to wait.

Hours later, as the afternoon was drawing to a close, Baba Yaga was awakened from a drowsy state by the sounds of an approaching horse. She sat up straight, for this was it—her chance to see if it was Koshchei and how he entered the pile of boulders. He finally came into view, that devil, astride his magnificent black *bogatyr* horse. She had to admit he looked impressive on it, the evil ogre in a man's form, filled with all the power he had acquired over the years and with all the confidence of being a deathless one. He looked not one day older than when he had first started visiting her when she was but a child. He dismounted and walked the few steps to the boulders.

Baba Yaga listened carefully to each phrase he spoke to the boulders and watched every motion he made, committing them to memory. When he stopped and stepped back, the boulders began to shift, and a large black hole appeared, an entrance. Koshchei strode through it and started to descend hidden steps with haste, and then he was gone from view. The boulders shifted back to their original jumble and became silent. She had it! At last!

The wait for Koshchei to leave was unbearable. How Baba Yaga wanted to rush down while he was in there and obliterate him with her magic and her anger. But she knew to be successful in rescuing Mariska that she must wait until he left. It was long after dark when the sound of someone whistling could be heard from under the boulders, drawing closer. Baba Yaga heard the same phrases and imagined the motions he would be using, and suddenly the boulders shifted and she heard Koshchei emerge from beneath them. He started whistling again as Baba Yaga heard him mount his horse and clatter away in the darkness.

She could wait no longer and moved quickly to the boulders, careful not to step on any traps or tricks that Koshchei may have left around the entrance. She muttered the phrases and made the motions, and the boulders parted before her. She felt her way down the first few steps until she could begin to see in the dim lighting, for more and more light was coming up from below as she descended. She began to wonder when the steps would end, there were so many, when they turned sharply and flattened out into the floor of a large room. This is where the light was coming from, as there were torches hanging along the walls of the room. Open doorways were seen around the walls of the round room, all of them leading into other rooms. Flickering light was coming from some of the doorways, darkness from others. Piles of rubbish and bones littered the far reaches of the room. Baba Yaga closed her eyes and reached out with her magic to feel if Mariska was here. She needn't have, for at that moment a sob was heard from the doorway to the right. Baba Yaga walked toward the doorway, half afraid of seeing her dear *vnuchka*, of seeing what Koshchei had done to her. She entered the room and didn't see anyone, just more piles of rubbish and bones here and there across the floor. Another sob was heard, and Baba Yaga realized that one of the piles was a girl in torn clothing lying on her side. The girl's back was to Baba Yaga, and so Baba Yaga had a moment to steel herself for what she might see. She walked over and gently touched Mariska on the shoulder, saying, "*Vnuchka*, I am here."

Mariska stayed on her side and began sobbing more, sure that this was yet another cruel trick of Koshchei's, for he had been having great fun tricking her in one cruel manner after another these past months. Baba Yaga gripped Mariska's shoulder and turned her over. "Mariska, look! It is your *babushka*, come to help you escape!" Mariska stopped her sobbing and looked at Baba Yaga through her tears.

"Is it you, is it really you?" Mariska whispered hopefully. She reached out and touched Baba Yaga's face and then drifted into unconsciousness. Baba Yaga only allowed herself a moment to look upon what had been done to her *vnuchka*, and thankfully the dim light kept her from seeing the worst of it. Baba Yaga had no idea how much time she had, for she didn't know when Koshchei would return. She picked up Mariska and slowly headed for the steps. But when she turned sideways to cross over the threshold of the room and enter the stairway, Mariska's body was jerked out of her arms by something invisible and hit the floor with a thud.

Magic! thought Baba Yaga. Of course Koshchei would have protections and defenses around a place like this, both to keep young women in and to keep heroes from rescuing them. Baba Yaga picked Mariska up, carried her back to the room, and laid her down gently. She strode back to the doorway and spent hour after hour testing Koshchei's magic, trying to work her magic around his enchantments, to no avail. All this time Mariska stayed unconscious on the floor in the other room. Baba Yaga decided to leave at last before Koshchei returned, letting Mariska think she had just been a dream. She would have to find another way.

Baba Yaga crouched in the bottom of her mortar, thinking and remembering. Perhaps the best, and possibly easiest, way to rescue Mariska was found in the stories that the *babushka* had told her long ago in her mother's village. She would find and destroy his soul. To do this, she would have to travel to the island across the sea where Koshchei's soul was stored in an egg beneath an oak tree. She could avoid a face-to-face fight with him this way, which, if she was being honest, she didn't know if she could win.

Once her decision was made, Baba Yaga set off in her flying mortar in the middle of the night, aiming it for the distant sea. All the next day she flew, crossing from land to sea at the rising of the sun and then continuing over the sea all day without the hint of any island. Then, just as the sun was starting its downward turn to meet the sea, she saw a speck of land in the distance. Soon enough the speck grew into a tiny island, empty but for a massive oak tree growing in the center of it. Baba Yaga was almost out of time, for the sun was now nearing the horizon. She got out of her mortar and walked around and around the base of the oak tree, reaching out with her magic to find the egg. Finally she felt where it was. In the growing dimness, for the sun had disappeared beneath the waves by now, Baba Yaga dug in the sandy soil with her hands, scooping and digging. At last she felt a smooth roundness, cold to the touch, for the evil in Koshchei's soul made the egg as cold as ice. She raised the egg into the air and looked at it for a moment in grim fascination. Then, as the coldness started to make her hand burn, she smashed it against the oak tree with all her strength. Great screams erupted from the smashed egg, and Baba Yaga dropped it on the ground and stepped back, covering her ears from the terrible sound. Wisps of black smoke drifted up from what was left of the egg into the ocean breeze and quickly disappeared as the screaming faded to a whispering sound and then died away. Now there was no sound but for the lapping of the waves on the island's edges. Baba Yaga realized she had been holding her breath and sucked in a big breath of air. Her thoughts turned immediately to Mariska, and she jumped into her mortar and headed out into the growing darkness.

Back at Koshchei's lair, he had just finished with his visit to Mariska and had paused while looking at her still form, trying to guess how much longer she would live and wondering why Baba Yaga had not come to rescue her. Ah, well, none of it mattered, he would use Mariska for what time she had left; he could get another young woman anytime. And if Baba Yaga never came to rescue the girl, he would just bring the girl's lifeless body to her hut and dump her in the yard beside the bone fence; then he would make Baba Yaga tell him everything he wanted to know about her magic. For never lived neither man nor ogre that was as arrogant and as evil as Koshchei the Deathless.

Just as he was turning to leave, the satisfied feeling that coursed through his body from his visit turned into something horrible, hot and cold at the same time, sharp, too, ripping and tearing through every muscle and bone, making him scream and scream as he stood there, ripping and tearing until it reached his head, shredding and shredding until his screams stopped abruptly and his body transformed into a thick black smoke which slowly fell to the ground and disappeared.

Mariska barely noticed the death of Koshchei in the half-dead state she was in. Everything seemed unreal and dream-like. Her mind had become blank as she counted each breathe, knowing one would soon be her last but having no feeling about it. Minutes or hours or days later, for time meant nothing to her anymore, she opened her eyes to see Baba Yaga leaning over her. "Babushka, Babushka," she murmured as Baba Yaga lifted her shoulders off the ground and tipped a warm liquid into her mouth. Mariska drank a few sips obediently, then drifted away into unconsciousness. Baba Yaga knew she had just made it in time; but for the herbs she had brought to make this potion and the magic to make it work, the deep sleep Mariska had just drifted into would instead have been death. Baba Yaga let go of her anger at her father, for she had killed him for his wickedness, hadn't she?, and concentrated on gathering up what was left of her dear *vnuchka* and heading home.

It took a very long time for Mariska to regain her health. All during the wet spring and the glorious early days of summer Baba Yaga nursed her body back to health, but she could only hope that the girl's spirit would heal as well. Mariska rested by the *pech* during the cool spring days, and Baba Yaga made a comfortable resting place on the porch of the hut once the warmer days of early summer arrived. Being outside, seeing the wild beauty of the yard and being visited by the birds and animals, this was what helped Mariska's spirit to finally start healing.

One summer evening, as the two women sat in silence on the porch, listening to the lovely sounds of the end of a forest day, Mariska said, "That's twice you have saved my life." This was unusual for Mariska to bring up her ordeal, for the women had decided early on to leave it in the past.

Baba Yaga Babushka thought for a moment, then replied, "No, *vnuchka*, it is you who have saved my life." The two women were the happiest women in all the land, for each had someone to love and to be loved by; they had found a family.

Many, many years later, as Baba Yaga neared the end of her days, she beckoned to Mariska, who was now much older herself. She placed her hands over Mariska's head and said the necessary words; her hands glowed, then Mariska glowed. "Mariska, my dear *vnuchka*, I leave everything I have to your care. Use the magic wisely and well. Now that I am gone, people may come to you for help, it will be up to you to decide if their reasons and intentions are to be rewarded, or not. You are a good woman, and the hut and all my possessions will serve you well. My dear *vnuchka*…" And Baba Yaga drifted off into her final sleep.

***

Jill Marie Ross lives in rural Pennsylvania beside a lovely pond with her husband, four children, three cats, and a sweet little dog. She is surrounded by books as a librarian, and she most enjoys reading and writing fantasy, paranormal, and historical fiction. She loves camping, hiking, and avoiding housework by curling up with a good book.

THE PARTISAN AND THE WITCH
Charlotte Honigman

When the witch opens the door, the girl greets her in perfect Polish.

"Dobry wieczór. Zgubiłam się w lesie. Czy mogę wejść?"

The words are raw ice and splintered wood in her mouth, but her accent is excellent. Probably much better than that of this old peasant woman in her house in the woods. You would not know that this is not her mother tongue.

In her last year of school, she won a medal for a recitation of a piece from *Pan Tadeusz*. Her inflections and emotions were so perfect that she saw the grammar teacher brush away a tear. It was only because of that old man, who was bitter and sarcastic, but always fair, that she even knew she had won. That fairness drove him to take her aside and tell her it was agreed that her piece had been the best, but that she would not be given the prize. It was awarded to the boy the judges gave second place to, a tall blond boy with broad shoulders, and parents who crossed themselves safely with the sun.

"You understand," he said, with his mouth folded tightly at the corners. "No one dislikes you. But it was agreed that the prize should go to a Pole." He nodded rapidly, as though to himself. "Still," he said, "you did well. Very well."

It should seem like nothing now, but the phantom heft of that elocution medal still weighs her pocket, along with a handful of other items remembered or imaginary. The hairpins she would lose by the dozens as a schoolgirl. The oranges that her *bobe* would buy her when such things still existed. The heavy brass key to a house in Palestine where she and Rywka will argue about politics and sleep tangled in clean sheets.

That elocution contest was two years ago, and even that recently, she had cherished some plans. She would go to university, somehow, and study agriculture. She and Rywka and Zivek would farm on a kibbutz near Haifa. There would be olive trees in the sun, and a language that was old-new and strong and did not leave splinters or phantom traces of sweetness on the tongue. But now her plans have come to this. She is standing in autumn woods, among birch trees, not olive or palm. She shivers in a rising night wind, and she stands before a fence made of human skulls.

Their eyes are alight, and they chatter at her from atop their posts with yellowed, weathered teeth, speaking no language that she knows. Skeletal hands clutch the long femur palings together. Fingerbones shift and twitch, clutching for purchase as the wind bangs the gate.

The house itself is an old farmhouse which looks as though it was once prosperous and cozy. Now its boards are scoured clean of paint by wind and rain, and there are dozens of shingles missing from its sharply pitched roof. The porch leans precariously. Smoke pours from the chimney, and is torn away by the chilled, damp gusts that set the carved shutters rattling like the teeth of the skulls.

The house roosts on its own legs, on the russet-feathered haunches of a great chicken, with its clawed feet clasped around a fallen tree. It is insane, this thing, all of it, but the girl no longer expects reason of the world. She has seen things that make less sense than this house.

She has spent a day in the forest now, watching the house. Lying low to the ground, she has watched it make its way around its yard. It acts like an ordinary chicken, and does much scratching at the earth, but it is mouthless and unable to peck at what it disturbs from the ground. She has watched it settle itself back onto its dead-tree perch, fluffing up the feathers of its legs. She has watched three riders gun their motorcycles up the narrow country road, watched the sun rise, and noon come, the day fade, and night fall. By the light of the fence's flickering eyes, at last she saw the witch return home in a wild swirl of wind. It's true what she was told, that the old woman flies through the air with a mortar and pestle to carry her. Now the girl stands before the fence of skulls, with her freezing hands balled in the empty pockets of her coat (too long for her, too large, it was Zivek's once, but though it is ragged, it's worn thin only in the elbows; a princely inheritance), and she takes a breath and addresses the old woman in her flawless schoolgirl Polish.

"*Przepraszam że Pani przeszkadzam,*" she says, "*ale widziałam że się u Pani świeci, a w lesie jest bardzo zimno.*"

Iz kalt.

"So it's cold," the witch says. (And yes, her accent is uneducated, her pronunciation that of an old country woman.) "What is that to me? I have a warm fire in my house."

She does. The girl can feel its warmth from where she stands, and it draws her numb feet closer to the gruesome fence. "May I come in? I have a favor to ask of you."

"A favor!" The witch's eyes narrow to a skeptical squint. "Why should I let you in if you're only going to ask me for a favor?"

She doesn't look as though she eats children, this old woman. She doesn't look as though she uses the bones of men to fuel her fire. She is stout and solid, massively bosomed and thick-waisted, in a housedress and a sweater. Her gray braided hair is tied under a kerchief like any farm wife. She has a face like a dried apple. Her faded blue eyes are colder than any the girl has seen, though, and this girl has not lacked opportunity to see cold eyes. Not the eyes of the malicious killer, nor those of the empty functionary. These eyes see dispassionately through the clear glass of the past and future, caring nothing for what they see. There is no love or hate in those eyes. No humor. No fear. A mind as isolate as the wind tossing the birch trees or the snow lowering the sky. What will be, is, those eyes say, with grim clarity. Whatever that might be.

In the harsh searchlight of those eyes, the girl repeats her request, quietly. "I would like to come in. I have a favor to ask. The woman at the farmhouse by the bend in the river said that you might be able to grant it. She showed me the path."

And she has to wonder now, did the woman at the farmhouse send her because she truly thought she might find help here, or because she preferred to throw the Jew to the witch rather than to the Germans, so solving her problem while keeping her family safe from notice? Or because she needed the girl gone, and agreeing to show her the way to the house in the woods was easy, no matter what happened after? What was she thinking when she sent her quiet, pale daughter with the long braids to take back to the forest the last survivor of the three who had lived beneath the floorboards for a short season?

The girl had sat *shive* under that farmhouse, cheek pressed to the freezing ground, the rhythm of her anguish timed to the creaking of the floorboards overhead. There was, occasionally, something to eat, there was, occasionally, rain. There was always cold, and always the sound of the wind at night. It was at the end of seven days that the woman at the farmhouse came to stand by the wall and wring out her laundry, and said, quietly, "You'll go tonight."

The girl hadn't answered, so the woman continued, quietly, in the same rough accent that the witch now uses. "My daughter can take you back to the forest, in the back of the cart. She can take you up to where the road turns off, and maybe you can find the fighters there. I don't know anymore. But if you want…"

Silence smothered the air. "There's someone you could go to. She's not with the fighters, but she might help. My grandmother went to her for help once. And before her, they say, others went too.

"There's a price. Always a big price. But I know the way."

Sense would have had her take to the forest again. The memory of Zivek and Rywka's blood soaking into the dead leaves sent her following the silent girl with the lank blond braids down a twisting path, still assuming that at any moment headlights would come on, and she would see her own death. Even when she saw the fence and the gate, it didn't convince her. She has seen bodies piled, bodies burning, bodies used to fill deep scars in the earth. Men, and women and children, young and old, rich and poor. It does not seem at all improbable that the Germans would have built something like what she sees before her. It is only the house with its nervous chicken legs and chicken habits that convinces her at last that she is in the presence of something more than another remote killing place.

The farm woman's daughter whispers good luck, and shoves something into the fighter's hand. Half of a thin slice of bread, gone stale. A parting gift, and hard to spare. The daughter crosses herself with the sun as she retreats back to the road, and the land of the living.

And now, as she pauses at the door, the girl wonders—was this the mother's way of making sure that no evidence of her aid to the fighters is left behind? Does she end tonight in the witch's oven, her bones added to that fence and the last evidence of the three of them erased? Nothing would remain, then.

In a world where life and death rest in the lightest of balances it hardly matters anymore. "I would like to come in and speak to you," she repeats, meeting the old woman's eyes. Zivek would have said it with his hand on his Nagant, but she has no weapon anymore.

There is a long pause, during which the girl shivers, and the witch waits, and finally the old woman snaps "So come in, then!" and stands aside from the door. The gate of bones swings open, and the girl makes her way to the threshold of the house.

Inside, she stands stunned. There is light, and heat inside the chicken house, more of it than anyone has had in years. The room swims with the smell of cabbage and potatoes rising from steaming pots on the old iron stove, and there is a blue and white china bowl full of oranges on the table. Overhead, there is a rustling and murmuring of pigeons in the rafters of the too-high room—it is high as a chimney and as narrow as a chimney toward the top—but below all is tidy and elegant and surreal. A shabby red velvet couch is draped with doilies and peasant embroidery, and an old Chinese rug lies on the battered floorboards. There is a canary, caged in brass that's been polished to shine like gold, singing away in the warmth of the kitchen.

It is the oranges that dissolve the last mouthful of skepticism that she carried past the chicken legs. This place is impossible. No one has so much food, or such food anymore. No one has food. Her head spins momentarily with the intoxicating splendor of it all, before she gets a grip on herself. She is still a soldier, and this place is in no way safe.

"Hang your coat by the door," the witch instructs her. "Wipe your shoes, too. And come in if you must. Don't think of stealing one of my oranges. I see how you look at them."

"Of course not, *babcia*."

"Come here and let me look at you."

She stands in the middle of the floor while the witch circles her, going left, then right, reaching out to tug at a lock of her hair, fingering the crudely darned cuff of her sweater sleeve.

"You don't smell like a Pole," the witch tells her finally. "Not like a Russian either."

She has practice keeping her expression slack and indifferent while soldiers, peasants, even the *goyische* fighters, cursed the Jews to her face. This is nothing. She shrugs a little. "I slept in the forest. I smell like mulch."

"That too," the witch laughs, but she seems to lose interest in the matter of what her guest smells like. "So, not-a-Pole, not-a-Russian girl, what favor do you want? What brought you into the woods to find a poor old woman in her broken-down house?"

At last, that's a question she can answer. "Death," she says.

More laughter. "If it's your own death you want, girl, you didn't need to come such a long path to look for it. Death is everywhere these days, and it costs nothing. You can smell it lingering over the land. Why would you bother to come to me looking for death?"

"It is not my own death that I want." She carries that in her pocket now, with the hairpins and the keys and the medals. She chews her lower lip, preparing the words. She cannot take this by force. She can ask, she can plead and try to bargain, but she doesn't know what she will do if the witch refuses her. "There are three men in the woods."

As she speaks, the witch stops her swooping and circling, and stands very still. "Which three men? Name them to me."

She knows no names. "There are three of them, and they ride on the road. One is all in white. His helmet and jacket and clothes, and the machine that he rides, white as dawn, white as bone, and I have seen him at first light, at the end of the railroad tracks, counting which prisoners have survived the night, and which have perished in the darkness."

"I know that one," the witch says thoughtfully. "He was my man once, but he found other masters to serve. Very well then, he, and who else?"

"There's another, all in red. Man and machine, his boots and his hair as red as day or blood, and I have seen him in the light of day, burning bodies by the thousands, with the flames as red as he in the daylight."

"I know that one as well," the witch says, "And he too was a man of mine before he found other masters to serve. Very well then," she says. "And the last one?"

The witch's eyes are cold as the dawn sky in winter when she says this. She already knows what the girl will say, and the girl knows it.

"He is all in black, man and machine, his clothes and all about him, black as night and the burned-over earth, and I have seen him in the night, hunting in the darkness. There were three of them that found us, three of them who killed the two dearest to me, and I want them all dead, but that one most of all."

"*Znam tego mężczyznę*, I know him as well," the witch says. "He rides at nightfall, and he was mine as well, once. Once, an old woman ruled more than these woods. So, say what you want with these men."

"I want to kill them."

There is a pause, and then the old woman bursts out laughing, genuine laughter from deep in the belly rocking her stout body and screwing up her wrinkled face in mirth. The girl stands unmoved, while the woman before her laughs until tears run down her sunken cheeks.

"Do you know what you're asking for?" the witch asks, smiling, when she has caught her breath. "No, you don't," she adds instantly, cutting off any response the girl might make. "You don't know. What do you imagine you're going to kill them for, for revenge?"

Nekome. The word warms her.

"Yes, revenge. And to save some who still live, if I can. But ordinary weapons don't touch those three. I saw that, when they killed my friends. We were not unarmed. We fought. Bullets do not touch them, they don't shed blood. The woman at the farmhouse thought you might have weapons that will harm them, weapons that will kill them, and if that's true, I want those weapons."

"I don't give things away," the witch says. "The woman at the farmhouse told you that as well, didn't she?" Her smile is unpleasant now. "What do you have to offer me in exchange for such valuable weapons, if there are such weapons?"

The girl had turned that over in her head as she lay behind the hedges, watch the house turn and scratch and settle. "I will work for you. I can clean, and cook. If there's any mending, I know how to darn, and do simple sewing. I can work in your garden, or do anything you need around the house or the yard. I can bring water from the river, and cut wood from the forest for your fire."

It seems so little, and so into the witch's pause she puts something else. "And I can do whatever work those men did for you once."

That provokes another short burst of coarse laughter, making the old woman's eyes crinkle at the corners in an almost human way. "You can't do that, girl, unless there's far more to you than even I smell. Tell me, though," and she pauses and smiles an old woman's sweet smile, "if I asked you to run and fetch supper for me—a child perhaps, to roast in my oven—what would you say to that, not-a-Pole, not-a-Russian girl?"

It's the first time the witch has said something perfectly witch-like, something grotesque to match the clattering gates of bone and skull lanterns past the door. And gliding like sharp skate blades on black ice, the girl's mind goes to the family at the farmhouse, the two smallest children, the son and the granddaughter, sitting by the fire, wrapped in what blankets there are, and savoring soup that is mostly water.

Those small fragile lives curled in their blankets like eggs in a nest are at once so vulnerable, and yet so much safer than any child of her own people. And she considers them, and the eyes of the witch with care before she answers with cold venom. "I would tell you that I can take you to a place where more children than even you could eat have already been given to the fire. You don't need me to go in the night to snatch any more from their beds."

"And if I said that I wanted you to go and snatch them from their beds nonetheless? And bring them to me? Maybe not the children of that woman who showed you the road, for her family is my concern. Some other child. A small price to pay, in times like these, and that is the truth, girl."

The truth is that she would crush those frail, cold eggs and never flinch. But she knows that, even now, Rywka would spit in the woman's face. It is for Rywka's memory, not for the children in the farmhouse that the girl shakes her head.

There is silence after that, with their eyes still locked, and she recognizes that their negotiation, such as it was, has fallen through. She won't let herself feel regret or uncertainty, not now. The witch is a dead end, so she will move on. She'll find another path to revenge, or die out there in the forest darkness before she reaches her goal.

She is turning to the door when the old woman finally reacts to her words, but it is only to shrug. "Hmmmm. I see then. Well, all right, keep your principles. I'll take it out of you in work," she says, almost mildly. "You can make the tea now. A strong cup of tea. And get me some cookies. Tonight you'll serve my supper, and then we'll see how you do tomorrow."

And with a curt wave of a hand, the girl's work is commuted from murder to kitchen drudgery. With her stained sleeves rolled to her elbows, she builds up the coals in the samovar, and brews the tea. She brings the cookies on a flowered china plate, and finishes cooking the supper simmering on the hearth. She dishes up the cabbage and potatoes, and washes the dishes, and throws the dishwater out the back door, in the direction of the skulls that still glow in the darkness.

She doesn't take off her shoes that night. She sleeps on the floor before the old woman's brick stove, in her coat, as she would in the forest. She does not expect to sleep at all, and she wakes a dozen times, each time startled again by the weird shadows of the witch's kitchen. At midnight, though a clock chimes, and the canary in its cage begins to sing, and before she can struggle to stay vigilant, she falls into a sleep as deep as a well.

She wakes before dawn, as the witch drops two heavy galvanized pails on the floor with a clang and thud. "Get up then. You've lazed about long enough. Get water and be quick with it. The pump is round by the tailfeathers."

She is filling the pails with water when the white rider goes by. The sound of the motorcycle's engine brings her head up, her blood thudding hard, but he goes up the road, past the gate of bones, without turning his head, and as the ghostly white of his helmet and jacket disappears among the birches, dawn breaks.

She brings the water to the kitchen, scrubs and boils. She makes breakfast, the smell of the food almost making her black out. She's startled when the witch thrusts a buttered heel of bread and half a potato at her. "Eat that, before you put me off my own food with your big round eyes." It's unfamiliar food now, even this scrap that's four times as big as what the farmer's daughter put in her hand. Most of what they eat in the forest is what they can hunt and forage for, rabbit and pheasants, or the mushrooms Zivek liked to cut with his knife from the earth, bunches of herbs simmered with the forlorn hope that there is any strength in them. She eats it as slowly as she can bear, willing her body to absorb it all, and then does the dishes while the witch sits at the table and drinks a cup of coffee through a lump of white sugar, and eats an orange, peeled with a silver knife. She may talk like a peasant, this old woman, but she lives like a rich woman in Vienna might have, once upon a time.

"Today is Monday." the witch says when she is done, "You'll do the wash." She nods, and follows the old woman to the stream by the house. If it's only laundry, she can manage.

But it's not one old woman's clothing that overflows the basket on the bank. It's stranger's clothing, women's and men's, children's, expensive and cheap, modest and modish, made of heavy gabardine and thin cotton, sturdy serge and flimsy crepe de chine. All of it is crumpled, all of it torn, all of it stained and caked with blood and smoke. There is more of it than she can believe, a mountain of *shmattes*, smelling of death, raised to the sky.

"Wash these clothes, and let them dry; mend and iron and fold it all," says the witch, her blue eyes alight with amusement. "Be done by the time I return tonight." And with that she mounts up on her mortar and pestle, and drives away into the autumn woods, in a great stirring of wind and wild leaves.

The girl is beaten, and she knows it. But she still picks up the first garment she sees. It's a child's sweater, small, and knitted by hand in a cheap scratchy wool the pale yellow of a winter egg's yolk. Half-dried bloodstains soak the back of it, with the singed edges of three bullet holes punctuating the tightly purled language of the yarn. She does not let herself think or feel, but simply plunges it into the icy water in her washpan. Soap and soda, washboard ridges and the strength of her own hands, and the blood washes out impossibly clean, swirling away into the clear icy water that runs at the bottom of the hill. She wrings out the little sweater and lays it on the grass to dry, and takes up the next garment, a man's work pants splashed in mud, one leg caked with gore.

Her hands are numb. She can't tell how much there is, and it seems as though there is never less, maybe more. She knows that no matter how long she works, there is no chance of being done with the washing. But she works and works, until at last she can no longer feel to grasp the clothing.

The red rider guns by the house, then, and disappears among the yellow-leaved trees, and the sun shines something warmer. The girl watches him go until the sound of his motor dies away, and then she dries her hands, and tucks them into her pockets.

Her fingers brush the edge of a photograph, and she pulls it out for a moment. Rywka's face smiles at her over the barrel of a rifle, and just for a moment, those reckless eyes are alight again for her.

She turns, then, as she hears a familiar tune hummed behind her. "Rywka," she says. "I'm sorry. I can't do what she wants."

Rywka's smile is as wry as in life, her freckles as stark on her pale skin, and her braids are loose over her shoulders. She puts a hand on the girl's shoulder, and leans in for a kiss, as casually as she might have done it around a fire in the forest. "*Chaja, meyn Chajaleh. Shlofn itst, meyn tayer. Sleep, neshomeleh,*" she says. Her shoulder, when the girl's face comes to rest on it, smells of sweat and sap and loam, and her arms are strong.

When the girl wakes, warm in a pool of unlikely sunlight falling between the trees, Rywka is gone, and there are baskets of laundry by the stream. Washed and dried, mended and ironed and folded. The yellow stars have been taken from each shirt and coat, leaving no stitch marks or faded patches behind. They float on the surface of the water like fallen birch leaves.

***

The witch's mouth is tight and irritated. "You had help," she snaps. "You could never have done all of that on your own." The girl looks back at her blandly. "Well, it's all done, so I guess it's no matter," the witch says at last, begrudgingly, "and it had piled up, no doubt. Come in and make my dinner. You've earned yourself one death today, and tomorrow we'll try again."

The two of them are awkwardly dragging the baskets of washing up the back stairs when the sound of a motorcycle's engine echoes from the road, and darkness falls. From the porch, the girl watches his lights recede like baleful stars into the night woods. The witch slams the door firmly behind them and bolts it. Her lips are tight, and she complains as the girl washes the supper dishes.

The girl sleeps before the stove, again, and as fitfully as before, until midnight comes, and the canary begins to sing. Then she sleeps like a child in a grandmother's feather bed, and she dreams of Rywka's lips until the witch wakes her again before first light. She fetches the water, watches as the white rider brings down dawn on the house, makes tea. "Today you'll clean shoes," the witch says when her breakfast is done. "Follow me."

Piled by the streambank, this morning, there are shoes. Thousands. Perhaps millions. The air is heady with the scent of shoe leather. There is mud on them, and blood. The high heels of women's pumps are broken. The strings of children's school shoes are frayed and knotted. There are workmen's boots that have walked in hell, and ivory satin bridal slippers that look as though they have danced in a slaughterhouse. They rise in mountains. "I want these put in pairs, each one cleaned and polished," the witch says. "There are rags in the box over there. Be done by the time I return tonight."

She leaves, and the earth shudders as she flies away on her mortar and pestle, and the girl is left alone.

She cleans and shines, scrapes filth away. Her fingers press through soles worn to paper. Blood and mud and shit, crushed bone and brain all coat the shoes, and though they come clean, disturbingly clean, under her rags, there is no end to them. She tries to sort, boot to boot and shoe to shoe, women's and men's and children's from one another, but the task is beyond beginning, let alone ending. The day is endless, silent but for the leaves, and the long approaching drone of a red motorcycle on the road beyond the house. Surrounded by the footprints of the dead, she sits down and touches the edge of the photograph in her pocket. Another miracle is beyond imagining, but she still lets herself whisper its name aloud. "Rywka? Rywka, *ikh ken nisht*."

She is afraid that this second time there will be no answer, but there is a footstep behind her. Rywka's hands are soft on her hair, and her cologne of sweat and woodsmoke hangs in the air. "*Keyn eyner ken, Chajaleh. Shlofn, neshomeleh, shlofn aun ton nisht khlum.*"

When she wakes, the shoes are paired, each with each, each shined and cleaned, with fresh laces and mended heels.

***

The witch's eyebrows gather together, gray and angry like stormclouds. "You never did that by yourself," she snaps. The girl looks up from lacing up her own worn boots, and says nothing. "Well, all right, then," the witch says at last. "Come in and make dinner. You've earned one more death today, and tomorrow we'll try again."

That night, as the golden canary in its golden cage begins to sing in the dark of midnight, the girl lies awake, unable to sleep. Maybe it's a few days of food and warmth disrupting the perfect balance of her indifference to life and death, or the memory of a young woman's brown hair. In the night she can hear a motorcycle's engine, and in the high feather bed with its embroidered covers, the witch mutters in her sleep. In the morning the girl stumbles through fetching water, cooking and sweeping, and waits, already exhausted, to see what the day will bring. The witch grips her wrist painfully as she leads her down to the stream once more.

On the banks of the stream mounds of ash and bone rise. The witch hands her a sieve from the kitchen, and their eyes meet. "It's the bones," the witch says. "I need them for the fence, you see. I plan to lay on a winter garden, and a woodlot. I used to have to add them one by one, but now, now I can have my pick, so long as I haul them here, and sort and clean them." She smiles, daring the girl to speak. "So this is all I give you for your third task. Sift the ash, and save the bones. Clean them and stack them for my fence, and you'll have the weapons you came for."

The girl does not flinch, but she sinks to her knees beside the mountain of gray death. The witch flies away with her mortar and pestle, the wild wind spraying ash through the autumn air.

It is beyond hope. Still, she begins. Slowly, methodically, her hands and clothes dusted and smudged and stained in death. She is surrounded by death, engulfed in it, breathing it. Her flickering life is an abomination before these remains, a child's toy in the ruins of a burned house, a crude joke spoken a house of mourning. Her hands are numb with cold, and the roughness of bone fragments, and she sifts and sieves without stopping, and finds nothing more than rubble under her fingers.

She continues throughout the day, until shafts of golden afternoon light illuminate the clouds of ash. When she finally begins to weep, her tears carve lines through the gray mask she now wears. "Rywka," she whispers. "*Ikh ken nisht.* There's nothing here. There's nothing left."

There is silence, and she sits for what seems like a long time, breathing in death, and wondering at her own tears. She has not shed them for much longer than she now expects to live. The *goyische* fighters would weep when they were drunk, sometimes, but the *yidn* locked tears away, and then their souls burned them dry. Perhaps, she thinks, it is only the eddying residue of the dead that makes her eyes water, the gray miasma that floats in the air of the golden afternoon.

The tears flow, but her voice does not catch as she speaks aloud again. "Rywka, nothing remains." She leans back into a sturdy shoulder, into warmth and embrace. Rywka's hair floats like the dust and ash, but her hands are steady and give comfort, and her voice is like honey and lemon. "*You* remain, *neshomeleh*."

"For how long? And what can I do, alone?"

"I have no answer, *neshomeleh*. But sleep now. Soon it will be night, and you'll need your wits about you."

"She wants…she wants…"

"Bones for her fence. Skulls to mount on poles. That's not hard to give her, not these days."

"I can't. There is nothing here, there is nothing left…and even if there were, Rywka, Rywka, how could I do that to them? To stand in this place, forever, to be denied burial yet again?"

There is a gentle hand on her hair. "Some of us chose to stand guard forever a long time ago," Rywka whispers. "Some of us expected that our bones would remain in the forest."

***

When she wakes, there are new bones in the fence, and the stream runs thick and gray with ash. The water is singing a soft tune of death to itself in the slanting golden afternoon sunlight, and red leaves drift on the rushing water.

The witch is not pleased.

"You never did that yourself," she snaps. "You had help. You've had help all along. Where is it coming from, girl? Where?" She advances angrily, but the girl stands her ground by the stream. "You never said I couldn't have help," she says.

"Where's it coming from? That's what I want to know."

"What does it matter?" The girl is backed up to the edge of the gray water. "You got what you wanted. Give me what I asked for."

The witch's brown, lined face is dark with rage and blood. "I won't have secrets kept from me in my own home, girl." Her anger seems to unsettle the house. It fluffs its thigh feathers and shuffles about nervously. "Using the dead to work on the dead…did you think I wouldn't smell it? Did you think I wouldn't smell what you are?"

"What I am?"

The witch grabs her arm easily, though the girl could have sworn there was the length of a coffin, or two, between them. "Doesn't smell like a Russian," she snarled, "nor like a Pole. A little *żydowska* lost in the woods. But there's more to you than that. What is it? What are you carrying?" Roughly, she turns the girl right and left and yanks out the lining of her pockets. There is nothing there. "What is it? Tell me, or we have no more bargains."

***

On winter evenings, her grandmother would light for Shabbes before she was home from school. She would come home in the twilight, with her satchel heavy on her shoulder. The house would smell of *chulent* and soup, *kugel* and apple cake, and her grandmother's candles would already be burning on the sideboard.

She would put her books away, and be greeted with a kiss, and her grandmother's *broche*. First she would be blessed to be like the *emahos*, and then for the light of the *Eibishter* to shine on her. And her grandmother would tuck a drop of wine from the *kiddush* into her pockets, "so that you should always have a little extra when you need it."

It was hardly noticed. In school, she would find another pencil when she had forgotten one, another hairpin, a few *złote* when it was raining and she needed to catch the tram. Later, in the forest, she would find a last scrap of bread, a few bullets, a bit of cloth to bandage with. Small things. So small, and so needed.

She recovers the coat, and slides the photograph from her pocket, now. "My friend is the one who's done your work."

"She's dead," the witch says, and the girl nods stiffly. "But this is not her work, though she comes at its calling. This reeks of blessing and holiness, it reeks of a good woman's doings."

"My *bobe*'s." Distrust is a habit so deeply rooted in her, and it's hard to think whether telling the truth is in any way safe. She has no idea what kind of a lie would work, or whether a lie could work here. She is truthful now. "She would bless me every *Shabbes* to have a little extra. And I still have that, even now. Even here. And now and here that is Rywka's help, to get what I need from you."

She explains nothing more than that. She doesn't need to. The witch shrieks once, then backhands her to the ground. The wind is lashing the trees now, and in the kitchen, the canary is singing a high warning note again and again. The girl tastes blood as she struggles to get up, and then the witch slams her down again, thumping her head hard against the ground. "Do you know what you have done?" the old woman hisses down to her. "Do you know that your pious little blessing will draw those you say you want to kill, like an electric torch would bring down the Germans and their dogs in a dark wood? No wonder they circle at my gate, no wonder they slow those engines they ride.

"Get up. I'll get you what you've earned, for I can't get around that, and then you'll get out. Out past my gate, as far as your legs will take you. I am having no *żydowska* grandmother's blessing hanging around this place. I can't have you here."

"You're afraid," the girl breathes. A slow, strange, beautiful smile twists her mouth. "You," she laughs, nearly in tears. "You're afraid of them. The Germans, they frighten you too."

The witch slaps her. "Pull yourself together, girl. Not the Germans, you fool. But those three that you imagine you are hunting…they'd never come looking for you, one little *żydowska* more or less, what is that to them? But that thing you are carrying— that *blessing*," she spits out the word like a curse, "that will bring them. And I will not have them brought back to my door, not as they are now, girl. I can't fight what they are now."

"So give me what I want," the girl says, "give me what I've earned, and I will kill them before they reach your door, *babcia*."

***

The witch does not bother to pretend to think much of her chances, but she storms back into the house, and flings open the cupboards of her kitchen. A great pile of brooms and mops and buckets, flatirons and odd bits of crockery come flying out as she rummages. Finally, she finds what she is looking for, and shoves it into the girl's hands. "Cursed weapon," she snarls, "taken from a corpse, and given to one who is nearly a corpse to make more corpses. Take it and be damned, girl."

The girl takes the Nagant, as though it were a bride's bouquet, as though it were a child, and cradles it in her arm. "That is for one day's work," she says. "And you owe me three."

The witch throws her a belt of ammunition, the rounds as bright as gold. She slaps a pistol on the table. "Cursed weapons," she says, levelly now. "Taken from corpses. Given to one who is nearly a corpse, to make more corpses. Take them, take all of this and be damned, little *żydowska*."

The girl drapes the belt over her shoulder, and puts the pistol into the pocket of Zivek's coat. "That is for one day's work, and that is two days paid," she says. "You owe me one more. You owe me something that can kill the black rider."

"You can't. The living cannot touch him, and the dead can't kill the living."

"There is something that can kill him. There must be. Give it to me."

"If it were to be possible," the witch says, at length, "this is how it would have to be. He would need to be killed as day passed to darkness. First his body would have to die, and then his soul would have to be destroyed before it could come back to his body again."

"I know how to kill a man," the girl says. "How do you destroy his

97

soul?"

The witch leaves her chaotic cupboard half open, with weapons and mops falling out of it onto the floor, and goes into the kitchen, where she brings something down from a high shelf very carefully, with her hands wrapped in a tea towel. A china soup tureen. Cradled within are hand grenades. Three of them.

"The first one will throw him from the motorcycle," she says, "and his neck will be broken. The next will destroy the motor of his mount, and that will stop his heart. Do you understand?"

"I understand."

"Once his body is dead, you will need the third grenade. You will need to shatter his heart, but not the heart of muscle and blood. His true heart will only stop beating when it is taken from this world. *Taken*. Do you understand me, girl?"

The girl nods, as understanding comes to her. Her eyes are keen with intention. "If I die too, destroying it, he stays dead."

"Yes. So you see, little not-a-Pole, not-a-Russian, it is not such a good bargain for you."

The girl picks up the bowl with both hands, and clutches it to her, like a farm girl with a clutch of eggs to sell.

"*Es iz a gut gesheft*," she says.

***

She goes out from the witch's house like a bride going to the *chuppah*. The rifle hangs from her shoulder, and the pistol weights her pocket down. The grenades she carries with her, and one more thing as well. A gift. "You can take one of my oranges," the old woman said, begrudgingly. "I see how you look at them. A little extra for you. You're a hard worker."

"Thank you, *babcia*."

"Now get out of my house. They'll be here soon. If you fail, I'll put your bones in the fence, so it won't be a waste."

"Thank you, *babcia*."

"Don't be insolent with me, girl."

"Of course not." She has what she wants, and there are only seconds left to guard herself around this old woman. She can hold her tongue a little longer.

The skulls chatter and gibber as she passes the fence, and walks through the gate. She makes her way to the place where she watched the house, and watched the road. Soon it will be dawn. She lies with her weapons around her, and her cheek pressed to the decaying autumn litter of the forest floor, and she waits.

***

The white rider comes down the road at dawn, and in the first light, the girl shoots him from his seat. The sights of the Nagant are true, and her shot is sure. The motorcycle spins and crashes off the road, and the rider's deathly white jacket and helmet are stained with his blood, and the rich mud of the road.

In the dawn light, she rises and makes sure of his death, firing twice more into his head. His face is oddly ordinary. Stubble, and ruddy skin going pale in death. Just another German lying in the dirt. It crosses her mind briefly that she has ruined his skull for the witch's purposes, but she supposes that doesn't matter much. It's as the witch said. There are plenty of bones to be had.

***

At noon the red rider comes. The sun reaches its height, and there is a brief surge of warmth in the woods—something almost springlike—as the gunning of the engine reaches her ears. He is forced to slow on the road, as he sees an obstruction ahead. He is slowing as he approaches the body in the road, and the girl raises the pistol in both hands and fires.

He falls from the saddle, but is trapped beneath the motorcycle, and man and machine spin out in a widening, eddying spiral. She can't see the blood on his blood-red jacket, nor on the crimson sheen of the motorcycle, but he leaves trails behind him. Her shot was true.

Still, he manages to ride to his feet, and draw his own weapon. He fires, missing wildly, and from her bracken blind she shoots again.

There are two bodies in the road above the witch's house, and the girl takes the time to rest, watching the blustering gray sky through the hawthorn twigs above her head. She sings to herself, a little song her *bobe* would hum while she cooked and swept, and softly, softly, another voice joins her.

***

It's in the blue cusp of evening that she lays out her weapons, and loads the pockets of Zivek's old coat with the grenades. It's as the first stars begin to shine in the sky that she finally takes the witch's parting gift out, and digs a thumbnail into the yielding citrus skin. Such a precious gift, such a ridiculous extravagance. An orange from a witch's hand. She peels it, and eats slowly.

When she slides a section into Rywka's open mouth, her friend laughs at her, with a mouthful of sweet juice. "Chajalah, what a waste. As though the dead can taste oranges."

"*Es iz nisht veystad.*" She is sure of that.

She swallows the last golden mouthful, and grips the grenade. She leans her head on Rywka's shoulder, and their fingers intertwine. Down the road, she can hear the motor of the black rider.

***

Charlotte Honigman was raised on Russian fairy tales and World War II legends; the inevitable result of growing up surrounded by veterans of the Soviet Army with stories of the Great Patriotic War to tell. She is a history teacher, wife, mom, and rabbinic school dropout, as well as a writer who weaves Jewish myth and history into fantasy and science fiction. As C.G. Griffin, she is the author of *Last Mass*, a mystery novel set in Renaissance Florence.

THE SWAMP HAG'S APPRENTICE
Szmeralda Shanel

A while back, some place down south, in Mississippi or Alabama, or maybe it was Georgia, in a town not far from the swamps, a mother lay sick in bed with not much time left to live. Her dark eyes that once sparkled like the stars in the night's sky had grown dim, and her dark velvety skin had grown ashen and dull. Her husband and daughter, Queen, whom everyone called Queenie stayed by the bedside and prayed. They prayed not for a return of health, for she was way past hope for that, but instead for a gentle transition to the otherside. On her last night on earth, she gave her beloved husband a final kiss and asked that he leave her alone with her little girl.

"Come close now, baby girl," the mother whispered, "and don't you cry so for me child. You got to know that while it's true I will be gone from this world, your dear mama will never be too far from you, lovey. Now here, I have something for you." Queenie's mother reached under her pillow and pulled out a tiny doll that wore a yellow and black dress, a red apron, a red headwrap and red boots. The little doll had many small braids all over her head and each braid was dressed with small beads and shells.

"Now listen here, sweet Queenie," her mother continued, "this doll has been in our family for a long long time, passed down from mother to daughter since before slave times even. My mama told me that it was carried over by one of our people who was stolen from her village and put on the ship that came all the way from Africa. You keep her with you at all times, hidden away in your pocket. Never speak of her to another and never let another see her. Remember to feed her now and then and to give her something to drink. If you find yourself in any kind of trouble, you talk to this dolly and she will help make sure you turn out okay." Queenie took the doll from her mama's hands bent down and kissed her and with that kiss her mother released her last breath and passed on.

Though her mother told her she would always be close to her in spirit, Queenie still felt very lonely for her and there were nights when it was just plain impossible for her not to feel sadness in every bit of her soul. On those nights she lay in bed holding her dolly close and she would cry. One night, she was feeling this sadness and remembered how her mother told her to care for her doll. She got out of bed, got a piece of bread and a drink of milk for the doll and fed her.

Suddenly her doll's eyes began to brighten, she breathed in and out, then she looked up at Queenie and said, "Oh dear sweet Queenie, I know you are sad and lonely for your mama but you are not alone, I am with you now. Lay down and try to get some rest, tomorrow will be better." And it was.

Queenie's father grieved for some years but eventually there came a time when he was ready to remarry. He was a handsome man, and had a good job as a marine merchant so there were many fine ladies who would've had him for their man. He had his eye set on a certain widow in the town. She was a very pretty lady which is what first caught his attention but even more so, she had two daughters of her own who weren't much older than his Queenie. Queenie's father was sure that a woman with her experience in child rearing and keeping house would be a good mother for his little girl. The widow was happy at another chance of marriage, and accepted his proposal. They were married in a short time and she and her two daughters moved into their new home.

The widow and her daughters were quite beautiful, with nut brown skin and eyes golden like honey, but they were none at all sweet. They frowned down on Queenie who, like her mother, was beautiful with hair, eyes, and skin like the raven's wing. When her father was around they would make like they were good and kind to little Queenie, but when he was out of sight they pushed her around, called her names and made her do all the housework. They were just plain ole jealous and mean. They made Queenie do the most demanding chores, hoping it would cause her beauty to fade. They'd set her to do all the scrubbing to wear away her nails and make her soft hands rough and they made her do any labor that exposed her to the elements, hoping the sun and wind would dry out her hair and crease her skin.

But it was all to no avail, you see, 'cause Queenie's little doll was always by her side and Queenie fed and took care of her just like her mother told her to. The dolly would set about taking care of all the chores and while she did this Queenie would rest in the fields, eat fruit from the trees, learn the songs of the birds and grow ever more beautiful. Her stepsisters on the other hand, who started out as true beauties themselves, began to grow thin and ugly because of their spite and wicked ways.

Years went by and as the girls grew older, the men folk came calling, looking for a wife. They always asked for Queenie and Queenie's stepmother would always say, "Naw, Queenie is the youngest and she can't be married 'til the older girls are. So no use in you coming around trying to call on her."

Well it happened one day that Queenie's father had to set out to sea. When he left, Queenie's stepmother moved the family from the house they were living in to another house that was closer to the swamp. She did this because she knew that the swamp hag's shack was near the edge of the swamp and it was her plan to send Queenie out to the swamp to get certain works done in hopes that she would "accidently" come face to face with ole skinny legs who would eat her up, bones and all, on the spot. You see, swamp hags don't like folks poking around too close to their homes and they have been well known to punish those that they find doing it.

Each day, Queenie fed her dolly and gave her a bit to drink before they went out to complete her chores, which usually consisted of collecting certain plants that grew near the swamp and catching small fish that lived in the swamp. Each day Queenie would confide to her doll her fears about running into the swamp hag, and each day her dolly reassured her that she would be safe. She promised to tell Queenie where to go to get what she needed and to always make sure that she stayed well away from the swamp hag's shack. And she did.

Queenie's stepsisters got so mad at the fact that Queenie returned home each and every day, whole and unharmed, that all they could do was fuss around the house day in and day out. "Oh I'm so sick and tired of that Queenie walkin' round here like she hung the moon!" one would hiss. "Yeah, mama, you have got to do something about her, 'cause she is workin' on our nerves real bad!" the other would chime in. The stepmother told her daughters not to worry because she had come up with a new plan that would surely get rid of Queenie once and for all.

One night, the stepmother got ready for bed and put out all the candle lights but one in a room where all three girls sat. She said to them, "Girls, I am tired and going to bed now. Before we know it the cold weather'll be comin', so tonight, before you go to bed, there's work that each of you got to finish."

She told the oldest sister that she must prepare for the changing season by quilting a nice warm bed cover and handed her a needle for sewing. She told the middle sister, that she must prepare for the changing season by making some nice warm socks and gave her knitting needles for knitting. She told Queenie that she must prepare for the changing season by making a nice warm floor rug and gave her many scraps of fabric for braiding. Then she left the girls alone and went off to her room to sleep.

Each sister began her work but in not too much time, as they had planned, the oldest sister accidentally coughed on purpose and put out the candle.

"Umph umph umph, it's real dark in here, now somebody is gonna have to go to the swamp hag to ask her for fire," the middle sister said.

"Not me," said the oldest, "My needle gives me light, so I can see well enough to get my work done."

"I ain't going neither," said the middle sister. "My knitting needles give me enough light to see."

Then both sisters looked at Queenie and said, "But you can't braid no rug in the dark, Queenie, so you haveta go to the swamp hag and get some more fire." And they pushed her out of the door.

"Oh no!" Queenie cried to her dolly as they walked away from their home. "They sending me over into the swamp to get fire from the swamp hag, she's gonna eat me up for sure!" But her little dolly assured her that she would be with her all the time so she need not worry.

As they walked towards the swamp her dolly told her when to turn this way and that so that she stayed on the right track to ole skinny leg's shack. They got to the edge of the swamp and her dolly said to her, "Now step on this here big log, it'll carry us on to the swamp hag's shack."

Queenie followed her direction but when they began to move along, Queenie cried out, "Oh no! Dear dolly, this here ain't no log, it's an alligator!"

"Well now I know that sweet Queenie, but had I said step on the back of this here gator and it'll carry us on to the swamp hag's shack, you never would have gotten on and we'd still be standing back there trying to figure out another way to get to where we going."

They rode the alligator's back for sometime through the swamp, passing cypress and black gum trees draped in Spanish moss. The song of the swamp was loud and eerie, croaking, splashing, whistling, whispering. You better believe that Queenie was scared.

They went on and on for some time then suddenly passing them on the bayou they saw a white man dressed all in white rowing a white canoe; as he went by the day came in all bright. They continued to travel on and some time later, they saw a red man dressed all in red riding in a red canoe and as he passed them by the bright sun stood high in the sky. They rode on for a long time more and far in the distance they saw a most bizzare structure. "It's up there," the dolly said, and in that moment a black man dressed all in black rowing a black canoe passed them by and the sky turned black.

Before them stood the swamp hag's shack on great yellow chicken legs. Surrounding the house was a great fence made all of human bones, on the tops of each picket were human skulls. All different sizes they were, and some of the skulls were still wearing their hair. Each skull had fiery red eyes; the eyes burned bright in the darkness and stared fiercely at Queenie.

The shack stood up on those chicken legs and spun around three times, kicking and splashing swamp water then it sat down still with the door facing Queenie. As she approached the fence that surrounded the swamp hag's shack, the wind began to whip and howl and the tree branches clashed together. The whole swamp anticipated the arrival of the swamp hag and every creature in it shut up, there was complete silence. All that could be heard was that crackling wind and a high pitched screech that approached the shack.

Sailing through the sky and downward toward Queenie came the swamp hag, riding in her cast iron skillet, rowing herself with her large wooden spoon. Eyes cold, piercing and steely gray. Hair long, thick, matted snaky locks. Skinny, skinny, with wrinkled tough brown skin hanging thin on her bones. She's got a long pointed chin with whiskers, a large long hooked nose and iron teeth. She smiled real big and those teeth flashed in the moonlight. Swooping down in her skillet she snatched Queenie up by her apron strings, flew her through the chimney, into the house, and dropped her on the kitchen floor. Queenie lay sprawled out on the floor wide-eyed and terrified.

"So you've come to my home have you, child? What nerve you got coming here disturbing me and mine?"

"Muh'Dear," Queenie stuttered, and she got to her feet and bowed. "I've come because my family needs fire. Ours went out and my sisters sent me to ask you for help."

"Humph," the swamp hag said, sucking her teeth. "Okay then, since you here already I'll help you out with some fire but it ain't comin' for free. I have some work that I need taken care of around this house and if you get it all done I'll give you your fire and send you on home. But if you don't… I'm gonna eat you up, bones and all," she said and flashed those teeth again.

"Now, I'm hungry, go'on over to the kitchen and take everything I got in the oven out. Bring it over to the table so I can eat it." The swamp hag sat down and Queenie followed her instruction. She brought out plate after plate of food and the swamp hag ate and ate and ate and seemed to never get full, just kept on eating and eating. When she finally had had enough she drank three tubs of beer, burped, farted and went to sleep.

She left Queenie nothing to eat but a tiny bit of salt pork, a piece of cornbread, and the leftover juices from the greens. Queenie fed her doll, took a little for herself and tried to go to sleep. She did not sleep well though, she was too afraid not knowing what would happen to her, plus the swamp hag snored so loud that the windows rattled and the roof of the shack popped off the top of the house and fell back in place over and over again all night long.

When it was still dark the swamp hag gave Queenie a little kick. "Wake up. I'm going out now little girl, when I get back you need to have my place nice and clean, inside and out. I don't wanna see a bit of dirt or mess nowhere when I get back. You also need to wash my clothes and fix my dinner. Oh yes, and one more thing. Out on the porch you'll find three bushels of mayhaw berries. I need you to separate the good ones from the bad ones and to wipe each one down so there's not a bit of dust on 'em. And listen little girl, I likes my mayhaws wiped down *individually,* so don't get it in your head that you can get the work done quick by rinsin' 'em in some water. I can tell the difference so you better do like I say." And with that the swamp hag hopped in her cast iron skillet and flew up the chimney and went off to wherever it was she was going.

Queenie looked out the window and saw the white man dressed all in white on his white canoe pass by and the sky brightened into morning. She looked around the swamp hag's house and shook her head. It was a terrible nasty mess and she began to cry.

"Don't cry sweet Queenie, only give me a bit a water then you lay down and get some sleep, it'll be alright," her dolly promised.

Queenie did as she was told and when she woke up again the whole house, inside and out, was clean, and the swamp hag's clothes were washed and hung to dry. Out on the porch, the bushels of mayhaws were taken care of too. Queenie looked out at the swamp. Passing by dressed all in red in a red canoe was the red man, and the sun stood high in the sky. "Everything is done, Queenie," her dolly said. "All that's left is for you to fix the dinner."

Just as dinner finished cooking, the wind started to whip and howl. Queenie looked out the window and saw the black man dressed all in black in his black canoe pass by and it was night. The swamp hag swooped down the chimney and stood before her. "Well? Did you get the work done? I'll have no excuses either, it's a yes or no question. No ifs ands or buts, child." She rubbed her bony hands together and licked her greasy lips.

"Oh yes, Muh'Dear," Queenie replied, "everything is done just like you told me to do it."

"We'll just see about that," the swamp hag said and proceeded to look over things for herself. To her astonishment, all was done exactly as it should be.

Now, while swamp hags are a mean, nasty, scary kind of witch, they are also known to be fair and will keep their word, so after seeing that everything was done to her satisfaction, the swamp hag sat herself down and ate dinner without complaint. She even shared a little with Queenie.

"Okay, little girl, you lucky for now," she said, grinning and chewing with her mouth wide open, " but you can't go home just yet, I got more work that needs to be done. You'll do it tomorrow and if you get it all done I'll give you some fire and send you on home. But if you don't, I'm gonna eat you up bones and all."

When she was done eating she sat up straight in her chair and pointed a long crooked finger at the door and commanded "In now!" The door opened and the bushels of mayhaw berries flew into the room and onto the table. "My servants, my children, my companions, here now!" The swamp hag clapped and with that three pairs of hands appeared out of nowhere. "Take these here mayhaws and make em ready for jam," she said, and the hands quickly carried the bushels away. With that the swamp hag stretched, turned her back to little Queenie and fell asleep. Queenie fed her doll and lay down in a corner on the floor and listened to the swamp hag snore.

When it was still dark outside the swamp hag gave Queenie a little kick. "Okay little girl, today, before I get home, you need to have this whole house clean inside and out, wash my clothes and have my dinner ready by the time I get home. Oh and yes, out on the porch, there are three barrels of mud fish. I need you to separate fish from scale, and don't you lose not one scale you hear me? I need those scales for important business. And don't you leave one scale on not one fish, I likes my fish nice and smooth." And with that she hopped in her skillet and flew up and out the chimney.

Queenie stared out the window and saw the white man dressed all in white rowing by in his white canoe, and the sky turned white with morning. Queenie looked around the house and thought to herself, "Well, at least the house is still mostly clean from yesterday's work, there's only the mess from last night's dinner." But just as she had the thought the house stood itself up on those chicken legs and began spinning around. As it spun, things flew off the shelves and landed all over the house and dirty swamp water splashed into the windows creating a terrible mess. The house sat back down.

Queenie cried out, "Oh no!" But her doll only laughed. "My my, this swamp hag is really something else," she said. "Just give me a little water to drink, sweet Queenie, and lay down and get some sleep, it will all be okay."

When Queenie woke up, her dolly said, "Now all there is left for you to do is fix the swamp hag's dinner." Queenie looked out the window and passing by on the bayou dressed all in red, rowing his red canoe, was the red man and the sun stood high in the sky.

Just as Queenie finished up with the dinner the wind began to whip and howl. As the black man dressed in black rowing his black canoe passed by, the sky turned dark with night and down through the chimney in her cast iron skillet with her great wooden spoon came the swamp hag. She took quick little glances around the house and said, "Right fine, the house appears to be in good order, but I gots to check on my scales and fish." She smiled, licked her lips and went out to the porch.

"Is she licking her lips for me or the fish?" Queenie asked her doll. "Probably both," the doll whispered, and Queenie shuddered.

The swamp hag came back in frowning. "Shit," she said shaking her head. "Lucky again." She sat down at her table pointed at the door, commanded "In now!" and the barrels of fish bounced into the house. "My servants, my children, my companions, here now!" She clapped and out of nowhere appeared three pairs of hands. "Take these scales and put 'em away for my business then gut and smoke these fish," she said, and the hands quickly carried the barrels away.

The swamp hag sat down to have her dinner; she shared with Queenie and eyed her suspiciously. Queenie sat quietly and ate her food.

"What's the matter with you child, are you dumb? Why you just sitting there all quiet not saying nothing?" the swamp hag snapped.

"No, I am not dumb Muh'Dear, I just don't want to bother you when you trying to eat your dinner," Queenie replied.

"Bother me with what?" The swamp hag smiled and leaned in. "You have questions don't you baby girl? Something you been wondering 'bout since you got here ain't it?"

"Well, yes, Muh'Dear" Queenie said, "since I been in the swamp I saw a white man dressed in white in a white canoe, riding on the bayou, who is he, Muh'Dear?"

"Oh, well that is my beautiful bright dawn," the swamp hag responded.

"Yes and I've also seen a red man dressed all in red in a red canoe riding on the bayou, who is he, Muh'Dear?" Queenie asked.

"He is my radiant rising sun," the swamp hag responded.

"Also, Muh'Dear, I've seen a black man dressed all in black in a black canoe, riding on the bayou, who is he?" Queenie asked.

"He is my mysterious magical night," the swamp hag responded. "Come on now baby girl, what else? I'm sure you have more questions, don't get shy." The swamp hag smiled and leaned in even closer. Queenie was about to ask her about the three pairs of hands that appeared out of nowhere, but in her pocket the little doll started to jump up and down and Queenie thought better of it.

"No Muh'Dear, I don't have any more questions and thank you for answering the ones that I had."

The swamp hag frowned a bit. "Humph," she said. "You a lucky somebody for real lil' girl, 'cause I don't like nobody asking me about what happens *inside* of my house, that's my own business. If you had asked me about those pairs of hands you been seeing 'round here, they would have appeared and snatched you up like the bushels of mayhaws and them barrels of fish and fixed you to be my next meal. Ummmm and I would have loved eating you, bones and all…" A bit of drool slid down the swamp hag's chin as she licked her lips. "Sure enough you lucky… And how you come to be so lucky, baby girl?" the swamp hag asked.

"By the blessing of my mama and her mama and all our mamas before that," Queenie responded.

"Mama's blessings? What you mean by that child?" The swamp hag narrowed her eyes and smiled a bit. "Oh, I see… your mama did the work, did she? Lay a blessing on you huh? What she known for? She a two-head? She work the roots?"

"I don't know what she do…" Queenie said feeling thorns pricking all at her heart as she thought of her mother.

"Don't you start crying up in here," the swamp hag snapped. "I see now your mama done passed and ain't had time to teach you nothing, but she was doing the work alright." She stood with her hands on her hips looking Queenie up and down for a while before she sighed and said, "Alright, alright. You can stay on here for a while and I'll teach you a few tricks before I send you on your way since you motherless and clearly come from a line of workers. But don't think that means I like you 'cause I don't like nobody. So what you wanna do?"

"I don't know, my sisters need me to bring fi—"

"Child don't be no fool and tell me you trying to take fire back to them trifilin' heffas that sent you here to be killed dead. You staying 'round or not? You go, you gone, can't come back, so what you gon' do?"

Queenie waited for a sign from her doll before she replied, "Thank you, Muh'Dear, I will stay on with you for a while."

That night Queenie lay with her dolly. The swamp hag told her they would start their learning the next morning. "But why did you tell me to to stay here and learn when I got you with me for help all the time?" Queenie asked.

"There are things that I know and can do that she can't, and there are things that she knows and can do that I can't," she was told.

Lesson 1: Medicine

"It's somethings can be taught and others can't, you either have it or you don't." The swamp hag stood with Queen on a log. "Take this here whole swamp. I know every tree, leaf, root, herb, flower, rock, bird, bug, snake, rabbit—everything that's living round here. I know 'em all by name and can speak their language too. Now that ain't something that can necessarily be taught. Not everybody got a mind for memory, recognition or hearing and understanding the way other things speak. And it ain't no point in me trying to teach you everything 'cause can't nobody know all of what I know. But, I'll teach you a thimble's worth of what I got and you'll know a hell of a lot more than most folks out there and more than enough to take care of yourself."

The focus of the first lesson was medicine for the body. The swamp hag taught Queenie which herbs, roots, stones and such to use for sore muscles, colds, fever, swellings, stomach sickness, toothache, to stop bleeding and things like that. Queenie learned how to make a tea, ointment, salve, syrup, bath or rub. Once she got good with those things the swamp hag told her, "Okay little sista, now that you got a hold of that, Imma tell you something else, sometimes the sickness is physical, but other times it be soul sickness, meaning it's spiritual." Then the swamp hag showed Queenie which roots, herbs, stones, flowers and things to combine in a bath, a potion, a pouch or whatever to draw luck, to remove a fix or curse, to knock someone down or send them away, to get money, and to control another.

"There's also ways to use these things for getting attention from somebody you got your eye on but I don't have nothing to do with that ole mess. Ain't never interested me in the least. You what they call a pretty girl anyway so I don't reckon you'll have no trouble finding you somebody when you ready to."

Queenie was eventually sent into the swamp on her own to identify and gather the appropriate plants for healing specific types of illnesses. When she returned to the swamp hag's shack she made medicines for each ailment and the swamp hag tested them all. "Humph. Well alright little sista, you good at this." The swamp hag nodded and smiled. "Very good. Now last thing you got to know is this—some sickness be natural and some be unnatural. When the sickness is natural it be just that, come on its own from something you done like being out in the cold too long, not eating right or not watching where you step so you fall down and hurt yourself. With the natural sickness, you use this here kind of medicine. But then there be unnatural sickness, that happen when somebody wishin' ill on you, want what you got or doin work on you. That can also happen if you upset some spirit in nature or the spirit of folk who was once living, you see. When unnatural sickness happen, then you use the spiritual medicine. Sometimes spiritual sickness look like physical sickness. To know what is what, you got to know how to read the signs."

Lesson 2: This Means This and That Means That

"Now all of everything around you got something to say. Thing is, few folks can understand what's being said. Let's start with the birds." The swamp hag went on saying red bird mean this, blue bird mean that. Crow caw one time mean this, three times mean that. Critter with four legs passin' by, stand still and look at you, mean this. It see you and run back in the direction it come from, mean that. Fruit or nut fall from a tree when you pass by it on the left mean this, same thing happen but it fall on the right, mean that. You look up at the sky, see a cloud look like a boat, mean this, like a star, mean that. A flower, a hand, a book, mean this, like a bear, mean that. And on and on she went. This lesson continued for many days 'til one day the swamp hag said to Queenie, "Okay lil sister, let's see what you got. Go'on outside, see what you see, come back and tell me what it mean."

Queenie did as she was told, when she returned she said, "Muh'Dear, I saw a crow, he hopped three times, looked at me, and then flew away. I looked up at the sky when it flew and saw a cloud that looked like a key moving toward another cloud that looked like an arm holding a baby."

"Okay, now what all that mean?" the swamp hag asked calmly.

When Queenie was done giving her explanation the swamp hag said, "Well alright, you got a good mind for memorization, but you ain't got much in the way of interpretation, which means you can read a little bit but you ain't gifted in the ways of sight. Oh well, not everybody is a seer. Anyhow, you can do a little with memorization, get a yes, no, good, bad, this or the other type of answer to things. But you won't get all the details 'cause you ain't really seeing, just using what you memorized. Even so, a little bit of knowing is better than none."

Lesson 3: Dreaming and Flight

"Now this won't take long, 'cause I know even if your mama didn't teach you nothin' she at least taught you this much, you gots to pay good attention to your dreams. If somebody that you love come to you in a dream, tell you something, you best mind 'em. And in the dreams there are some signs too."

"I know some of it," Queenie said.

"Oh you do? What you know, lil' sister?"

"If you dream of fish, somebody pregnant. If you dream of a wedding, there's gonna be a funeral, if you dream of a funeral somebody getting married soon."

"Ha! Is that all you know? 'Cause that ain't too much," the swamp hag told Queenie.

"No mam, it ain't," Queenie said. "I get the numbers in my dreams, my old granny who passed on long ago comes to see me in them sometimes too. I dream things that happen later on, and that's not all, Muh'Dear."

"It ain't?" the swamp hag asked, grinning a bit, at Queenie's sudden boldness.

"No it ain't. I know how to leave myself and fly on off to see what's happening over in other places," Queenie whispered.

"Oh you know about flight do you, lil' sister? While you sleeping or when you woke?" she asked.

"Both," was Queenie's response. And at that the swamp hag smiled wide, flashing all those iron teeth. She nodded her head and said, "Very good, very good, then we done with the learning for today."

Lesson 4: To Visit With the Dead

"You don't always see 'em, sittin there right in front of you like we sitting here right now. Sometimes they come in dreams, other times you'll hear they voice, or smell the smell that was theirs all around you when they come. Either way, what I'm telling you today is that you don't always have to wait around for them to show up on they own, there be ways to call 'em to you. Now this ain't something that you do all the time or even just 'cause you longing to see 'em again. It take a lot on both ends for them to come back. It ain't easy simple stuff for us and it's even harder for them, so don't be selfish or foolish. Only call on 'em once in awhile and when you really need something."

Then very quietly, and slowly, and with something that almost resembled gentleness and care, the swamp hag taught Queenie everything she needed to know to bring on a visit from the dead. She then left her alone for several days to complete the test.

When the swamp hag returned, the signs of spirit visitation had left the shack filled with light. She knew Queenie had passed the test and was crying because she'd had a visit from her mama.

"You want to keep 'em here once you see 'em, I know. But it just can't be, Miss Queenie," the swamp hag told her.

Lesson 5: Workin' the Elements

"Alright now Miss Queenie, this'll be some fun 'cause it's one of my specialties. I'm gon' teach you 'bout movin' the winds, calling down rain, shaking the ground and making a spark. Now this the type of thing you gotta feel real close and deep. With your whole self you got to connect to whatever you trying to work. I been doing it so long it come easy to me, I want the wind to move I breathe in and then out and the wind already know what I want and agree to it. I want sparks I snap my fingers fast and a flame come up. I get deep into my bones and fix my eyes and the ground do a shuffle, move back and forth. I lift my hands upward toward the sky, drop my head back and call the rain right on down. You got to find your connection to these things, be with 'em, know 'em like somebody you close to and then you'll be able to work with 'em."

"Is that how Moses split the sea and Jesus calmed the storm and walked on water?" Queenie asked.

"*If* they really did those things, then yeah that's how they did it, be the only way for them to do it," the swamp hag replied.

The first week the swamp hag brought in great winds and left Queenie to work, eat and sleep in them. This is the way one learns the language and ways of the winds. The second week she left Queenie with flames and ember. The third week Queenie's companion was rain and the fourth week her teachers were stone, dirt and mud. When the day for testing came, Queenie could barely stir up a small breeze and could not make fire or bring the sun through the clouds. She could not move the land or even manage to make it rain, not even a drizzle, not even one drop, so the swamp hag didn't bother with making Queenie suffer and sink by testing her walk across the top of the swamp waters.

"Damn." The swamp hag scratched her chin and shook her head.

"You ain't no good at none of it. Oh well, don't feel too bad Miss Queenie, like I said in the beginning, not everybody can do everything. Weather work and such just ain't for you. Now, even when folks can do a lil' bit of this and a lil' bit of that, everybody got what be called a specialty. You just gotta find what yours is and put your heart and soul into knowing it inside out. It's something you got to find for yourself but I can tell you this, I suspect your specialty is healing. Still, it's many types of healing and if you a healer, you still gotta find out what your healing way is."

A Gift of Bones

The next morning, the swamp hag woke Queenie up at dawn. "Okay Miss Queenie, get on up it's time for you to be on your way," she told her.

Queenie got up quickly. "Oh, Muh'Dear, why do I have to leave? Is it 'cause I didn't pass my tests with the weather?" she asked.

"Oh no, naw, it ain't that, it's just time. If you stay here much longer you'll be 'bout as old as me," the swamp hag said. Queenie shook her head, not understanding. She was just a girl and had not been there for more than five or six moons. The swamp hag, seeing Queenie's confusion, pulled a small mirror from her pocket and held it before her. Queenie gasped; she did not recognize the face that stared back at her. In the mirror she saw, not a girl, but a young woman.

"Don't worry Miss Queenie, I have something here for you." The swamp hag put the mirror back in her pocket, then took out a small red pouch and handed it to Queenie. Queenie looked inside.

"Possum bones," the swamp hag told her. "If you need something from me, you take a stick, draw a circle on the ground in the dirt, ask your question, toss these bones inside, look at them, wait, listen, and I'll tell you what you need to know." Queenie took the pouch and put it in her pocket beside her doll.

"It's time," the swamp hag said. She stood on her porch, whistled and a giant alligator came to the edge of her house. "Big John," she said, "carry Miss Queenie back on to the mainland so she can get on home."

Queenie looked at the swamp hag, suddenly feeling a pain that she would never have expected and thought to ask if she could just stay there.

"I know you miss your mama, and you been here with me all this time," the swamp hag said, touching Queenie's cheek, "but you gots to go now and be in the world. You gon' be alright, you got the blessing of your mama, her mama and all y'all other mamas before that. You got everything that I taught you and if you need something else from me, something you ain't got right now, you got the bones I gave you."

Queenie wanted to hug the swamp hag, but she knew better than to do so. Instead she placed her hand upon the swamp hag's hand that still rested on her cheek and nodded before getting on the Alligator and heading home.

"Sit down," her dolly told her once they were on Big John. "There is nothing to be scared of, this gator knows better than to harm somebody that the swamp hag favor." So Queenie sat down and relaxed this time as they traveled through the swamp.

Once she reached the land, her doll told her which paths to take to get back to her house. When she arrived, the house was cold, dark and empty. So she continued to walk until she found a small town and there a kind old woman took her in, in exchange for some help around the house.

She was very happy living with the old woman, but occasionally she got bored with just cooking, cleaning, and sewing. She did not complain, but her dolly noticed something was ailing her. One day after eating a bit of food that Queenie sat before her she said, "Queenie, go out and fetch me one tall straight stick, a big ole pumpkin, and 21 hairs from a horse's mane, and I will make a special gift for you."

Queenie went out, gathered the things her doll had requested, brought them home, and went to sleep. When she awoke the next morning, she found her doll had made for her the most amazing stringed instrument. "It's called a Kora," the doll told her and she taught Queenie how to play it.

She got so good at singing and playing the Kora that people in town began to follow the music to the old woman's house just to listen outside. Eventually they started bringing gifts and money to the house just to sit inside and hear Queenie play for a while. Once inside folks found that Queenie's music *touched* them in a very powerful way. While one person listened to the music and felt heat, another felt a cool washing over them, another a brushing, another a lifting, another a holding. Word spread far and wide about the enchanting woman with the beautiful voice and the magical instrument.

"She's a healer," folks exclaimed, "healing with them songs she sangs and that funny instrument she play. She get started with that music and the spirit come right on down, you feel the hands laid on you just like you was in church. That music can lay a blessing on you, break a curse, tame grief, fix your money, draw sadness out your heart, fill loneliness with love, destroy hopelessness, give you strength, anything you need, you can get it when she playin' that music and sangin' them songs," the people said.

A woman who had never been blessed with children, but wanted them more than anything, heard all that folks were saying and allowed herself to feel hopeful. She gathered her courage and went to listen to Queenie play. As Queenie played and sang, the music rode the woman hard. First she jerked and trembled, then she got to jumpin' and shoutin' "Yes! Yes! Whooooo! Yes!" and danced herself on out the door. She danced up the street and into the town's little graveyard. Round and round she danced around her great grandmama's grave, she danced and shouted, and cried and prayed around it all night long. Nine days later her breasts felt swollen and tender. Nine weeks later a little bulge poked from her belly. Nine months later she gave birth to triplets.

Queenie had found her specialty, she knew it inside out, was doing the work and she was doing it better than good. It seemed that everyone knew of her music's ability to heal the afflicted, but what most people never knew was that her music could also punish.

One morning there was a knock on the door. Queenie opened it to find a woman standing there bent over and crying. "Miss Queenie," the woman said in a little bitty voice, "I'm sorry to bother you so early in the morning, and I ain't got no money to hand over to you, but folks 'round here say you got some kind of power and I need some help mighty bad."

Queenie invited the woman in. "Sit down now Ma'am, and let me fix you a cup of coffee," she told her. When she returned with the coffee and some biscuits the woman was no longer crying, but still looked very upset. "What is it that you think I can help you with, Ma'am?" Queenie asked her.

"The man I work for won't do right by me, Miss Queenie. I been cleaning his house all these years and for more than two months now he telling me he gon' pay me later, for two whole months now he ain't paid me none. I don't have much, and I take care of myself, nobody here to help me, my husband passed on years ago. I'm too old to find work someplace else, ain't nobody gon' hire me to do nothing, I'm not strong like I use to be, work slower now, and that no good evil like the devil man knows this. When I say something to him about my money he tell me if I keep making a fuss, gettin' on his nerves he just gon' let me go. He ain't no good, and mean too, 'specially when he got the drink in him, which is most times. He tell me 'Hazel, don't ask me about no money, I'll pay you when I got it.' Callin' me by my first name when I'm old enough to be his grandmama. Then he tell me, 'I only keep you 'round 'cause you raised up my mama and she loved you like you somebody important or something. I promise her before she died that I'd keep you in work. Wasn't for her I'da got rid of you long time ago and got myself a young gal in here who could do more faster and at least be something to look at.' He just low down, and I don't know what I'm gon' do, Miss Queenie, I need my money, I got to eat, I got to take care of myself."

Queenie went to the kitchen and packed a basket with eggs, biscuits, and ham. She brought the basket to the old woman and refilled her coffee. "Even with all I know how to do, I don't know what to do to help you in this situation, Ma'am. It ain't right and I wish I could do something, but I just don't know what I can do for what is happening to you, I am so sorry. I brought you these things though, and if you need something else don't be shame to come by." Queenie wrapped some coins tight in a handkerchief and added them to the basket. "I know he owe you much more than this, but I hope it helps you some."

"You a sweetheart and I appreciate your kindness and charity. I know can't nothing be done 'bout white folks doing wrong, guess I was just feeling hopeful after hearing 'bout your work and all." The old woman stood up to go and Queenie's little doll started to jump up and down in her pocket.

"Wait," Queenie said, touching the woman's shoulder. "I might be able to help you some more. Come back to see me in the morning." The woman nodded and smiled a doubtful smile, gathered her things and left.

"What can I possibly do for her?" Queenie asked her doll.

"You must call on the swamp hag. Throw the bones," her doll told her.

That night Queenie drew a circle in the dirt on the ground and tossed the bones inside. She fixed her eyes on the pattern that they made. "Muh'Dear? Muh'Dear?" She waited.

"Yes, daughter?" The swamp hag's voice came loud and clear.

Queenie told the woman's story and the swamp hag clicked her tongue and sucked her teeth. "Now daughter don't you act like I ain't taught you nothing. So you found your gift of healing come through your music, if you can sing a blessing, you gots to know you can sing a curse. Now, tell the woman to gather some dirt from the grave of that wicked man's mother. You gon' turn his own against him, get her her money, run him mad, and run him off. He is a low down somebody for sure and you gotta *fix* his ass. Now, when she brings you that dirt, you play your music over it three times a day for three months. Give the dirt to the woman and tell her to sprinkle it all around the house, in the house, on his clothes in the dresser drawers, and in his food. The spirit of his mama gonna wake up and she'll take care of the rest. When the work is done tell the widow to clean everything up real good, then visit the grave of that man's mama again, this time with a gift of white flowers and pound cake. That woman loved pound cake."

Queenie did as the swamp hag told her. After the dirt had been sprinkled in and around that house It took only a few days for things to start happening and less than a month for things to finish.

After taking the flowers and poundcake to the graveyard the woman stopped by Queenie's house to let her know what all had happened.

"First few days I notice he actin' kinda funny, jumping, looking this way and that. Then I hear him say 'Mama won't you stop fussin' at me? Stop fussin' at me mama, I'm gon' give Hazel her money.' Each day he getting worse, drinkin' more, talkin' to his mama like she standin' right there in front of him. 'Leave me alone mama! Let me be!' He steady sayin. He stopped eatin', stopped sleepin', walkin' 'round looking crazy, talkin' crazy, crying even. Then one day he come to me with all my money and say 'Hazel here, take it, please won't you just tell mama to go on back to the lord and leave me alone. She worryin' me worse than when she was livin'. I can't get no rest, she follow me all around this house fussin' at me 'bout how I treat you. I ain't treat you bad! Tell her I ain't done wrong by you so she leave me alone. She even followin' me to the bathroom. I can't get no peace, Hazel.' I just look at him and shake my head. 'Sir, I don't know what's wrong with you, you know your mama been gone for many years now,' I told him.

"Finally one day he come to me with all these little bags full of money, he say, 'Take it Hazel, take it all, I'm leaving, you can stay, the house is yours, I'm gon' leave and won't come back, just please keep mama here with you, don't let her follow me out this door.' Then he left that house and ain't been back since. Miss Queenie, the house I been cleaning all these years is mine now." The woman laughed and thanked Queenie many times, then handed her a lot of money and went home.

Queenie stayed in the town for sometime doing her work. The people loved her and she loved the people, but one day her dolly said to her, "Okay, Queenie, it is time for us to move on, there are folks all over this land needing your magic." So with her dolly in one pocket, the bag of bones in the other and her Kora in hand, Queenie set out to do her work in far away places.

In no time at all, Queenie became a famous healer-musician, and was blessed with great prosperity. She traveled the world healing people with song, found love wherever she went, and lived happily for the rest of her days.

***

Szmeralda Shanel is an expressive arts therapist and educator from Chicago, IL. She loves folklore and especially enjoys writing fairy tales that reflect the rich cultural traditions, practices and folk beliefs of African Americans.

BOY MEETS WITCH
Rebecca A. Coates

In the deepest, darkest part of the forest, where the trees grow as tall as the sky, there was a small clearing, and in that clearing was a single-wide General Coach "Chateau" trailer on cinder blocks. Its white sides were dull with dust, its window curtains were faded, and its awning dipped at one corner where the supporting post tilted like a drunk.

Alex pushed up his glasses with a knuckle and tongued his braces nervously. Maybe the kids at school had been having him on. Maybe they'd known he was eavesdropping and this was all a big set-up.

He'd left his bike at the base of the trail where it branched off the old logging road. Dry needles crackled under his sneakers as he picked his way across the clearing. The sun was bright overhead, but the trees were so close together that only a slender shaft of light, still hazy with smoke from the summer forest fires, broke through. A double line of round white stones, half-hidden under dead twigs and snarls of browning ferns, led up the front path. Beneath the trailer's front door, three aluminum steps dangled over the dirt. They echoed tinnily under his feet. Heart thumping in his throat, he raised a hand and knocked.

No answer.

"Hey! Anybody home?" He knocked again, harder this time—
bang! bang! bang!

The trailer trembled with approaching footsteps. The door flew
open, and an old woman glared at him through the screen. She had a
bird's nest of dirty white hair and a wobbly jaw like a hound dog.
Spotted pouches sagged under her watery eyes. Her whole face looked
like it could slide off its bones as easily as an egg out of a frying pan.
"Vat da hell do you vant?" she said in an accent like a B-movie
Dracula.

"I—" His voice cracked embarrassingly. "I heard that, uh, that a
witch lives here."

She raised one hairy white eyebrow. "So?"

"I need your help." He shoved his fists into his jeans pockets and
shifted his weight from foot to foot. "I need you to, um, take care of
someone for me. You know, like *take care of*?"

The old woman narrowed her eyes. "Go home, little boy," she
said, and slammed the door shut.

He flinched. *Rude old bitch!* He was 14! He wasn't a *child*. He
banged on the door with his fist, shaking the frame. "Hey! Hey, lady!
C'mon, please?"

The door opened just enough for her to squint through it, looking
him up and down. He was taller than her but only just, still waiting
for that growth spurt he really hoped was around the corner. She
sucked on her teeth, which were white and weirdly even. Probably
dentures, he figured; it would explain why her *s*'s sounded so mushy.
She licked her creased lips. "You are fat enough, I think."

His face went hot and he had to bite his tongue, hard, to keep
back something rude.

"Well," she said, "maybe I will help you. And if not, you will
make nice meal."

"Yeah," he said doubtfully, "I'm not much of a cook."

She wheezed out a laugh like he'd just said something funny.
Witch or not, he decided, this old bag was seriously wacko.

She stepped away from the screen door and shuffled into the trailer. Her red velour track suit was stretched and shiny across her lumpy bottom, which seemed to have sucked all the flesh out of her arms and legs. "Don't stand in doorway," she said without turning around. "Come in."

The place smelled strange, musty and sweet. Dusty maroon carpet covered the floor and also the walls, where it clung like some kind of mutant moss. The kitchen cupboards and the small fold-out table were colored to look like dark wood. To the right of the table, a sofa had been built into the end of the trailer to suggest a living room. To the left, beyond the kitchen, a curtain blocked off what had to be a bedroom. Tacky little figurines cluttered every surface: ceramic ballerinas in mid-pirouette, corn husk dolls, fishing gnomes, big-eyed kittens with balls of yarn. It looked like the world's worst yard sale.

"Sit," she said, pointing at the cramped sofa. He slouched onto it and waited, jiggling his leg.

The old lady went to the kitchen and started fiddling with a weird contraption—a huge, seething pot that crouched on the counter on fat little legs. "What is your name, boy?" she asked, not looking around.

"Alex. Alex Rusnak."

"Alexander?"

He watched as she turned a spigot on the pot-thing and a stream of steaming liquid fell into a mug. "Yeah," he said, "but nobody—"

"I will call you Sasha."

"That's a girl's name!"

Turning from the urn, she gave him a withering look. "In Russia, Sasha is short for Alexander."

"We're not *in* Russia, in case you haven't noticed." *What a relic!*

The wind must have picked up, because the trailer creaked and swayed a little, and it seemed as if a cloud passed over the sun. He squinted, pushing up his glasses.

The old lady frowned at him. She had a really impressive frown, like something out of a horror movie. "Lucky for you that you are fat."

"Give it a rest!" he muttered, flushing.

She carried over two steaming, mismatched mugs and set them on the table, then took a seat herself in a creaking chair. "Here," she said. "Drink tea now."

The tea smelled rank, and there were little flakes floating in it. "Do you have any beer?" he asked hopefully.

"No beer," she said. "Only vodka. Vodka is for me."

There was a can of orange pop in his backpack, left over from school. It was warm and fizzy but better than nothing.

They both slurped at their drinks, the woman holding her mug in both hands. Her fingers were twisted like tree branches, the nails long and yellowing. "So," she said, setting the mug down with a tap. "Who do you want me to kill?"

He nearly choked on his pop. "Not kill! Just, like, make him disappear or something."

"Who him?"

"Matty Kravchuk," he spat.

"And who is this Kravchuk?"

Alex slumped down in his seat and picked at an unraveling thread on the knee of his jeans. "He's a dick. I hate him." Matty Kravchuk: rich kid, hockey star, all-round douchebag, with his stupid spiky blond hair and his better-than-you smirk. "He's always picking on me. Calls me names and stuff." *Get out of the way, loser!* he'd shout before body-checking Alex into the lockers. Alex scowled down at his jeans. "You know. Throws stuff at me, takes my glasses. Thinks it's frickin' hilarious." It wasn't like Alex'd been super popular at his old school, but here in a new town, with no friends, he had suddenly become easy pickings.

"I see," said the old woman. "You have tried talking with him?"

He rolled his eyes. God, adults were stupid! Dad was always saying stuff like "Stand up to him! Bullies are cowards. Once he sees you're not a pushover, he'll leave you alone." Somewhere in Dad's brain there was a picture of Alex labeled *My Son: The Pushover*. The teachers were no help, either. They'd tell Matty to cool it, then turn a blind eye. What they really meant was "Don't do anything where I can see you and would have to do something about it." Matty's dad was the town's police chief, and none of the teachers wanted him to turn up and start shouting at them for making his son miss hockey practice. It was easier to blame the new kid for being a spineless blob. "Be a man!" Coach Campbell had once said to Alex when he complained after Matty nailed him in the face with a dodgeball. He'd had a black eye for a week.

To the old woman he said, "There's no point trying to talk to him. The guy's an A-hole. He's never gonna leave me alone unless I do something to make him. That's why I need you. I have some ideas," he added, digging into the front pocket of his jeans. He pulled out a much-folded piece of notebook paper and spread it open on the table. "I don't know how your—" He waved his hand vaguely. "—*thing* works, so I figured you could choose whatever seems best to you."

"Thank you," said the old woman drily.

Leaning forward, he read, "One: Make it so I know kung fu. Like, maybe you could download it straight into my brain, *Matrix*-style. And then I could kick Matty's ass."

"You want to kick ass."

"Yeah."

She sipped her tea. "This will not solve problem."

"What do you mean?"

"Will not get rid of Kravchuk boy. He will only turn on someone else."

He scowled. "So? That's not my problem."

The old lady said nothing. She rummaged in the pocket of her track suit and pulled out a small pipe—bigger than a pot pipe, but not one of those huge Sherlock Holmes things—and a tin of tobacco, ignoring Alex.

"Fine! Forget the kung fu. Option two: Give Matty some kind of disease, like mono or AIDS or something. Nothing fatal, but bad enough that he's too tired to mess with me. Or, even better, he'll be too sick to go to school. How about that?"

She unscrewed the tin, snagged a clump of tobacco, and pressed it into the bowl of the pipe with her thumb. "Would be easier just to kill him."

He winced. "Enough with the murder, okay? Calm your t— self."

"Catch!" she said, and a book of matches came sailing at his head. He tried to catch it one-handed, but it bounced off his palm and landed on the table. On the front it said *Glenda's Diner* in pink neon letters. "Light," she demanded.

Rude much? he thought, fumbling with the matchbook. He had to strike three times before the match caught. At her gesture, he held it over the pipe bowl while she sucked and puffed. In a minute the tobacco was glowing on its own, and a heavy, sweet scent filled the trailer—the weird smell he'd noticed when he came in.

He picked up his paper and pointedly cleared his throat. "Three: make one of the popular girls go out with me. Like Stacey Minchev and her crowd. You know, the pretty ones."

The old lady raised her hairy eyebrows at him and smoke crawled out of her nostrils. She looked like a smaller, nastier Gandalf.

Clearing his throat, he explained, "'Cause then I'd be popular too. And if Matty tried to give me grief, everyone else would be mad at him." It wasn't like he had no friends—there were still his friends back home. He talked to them online all the time, playing World of Warcraft or just watching videos together. But as far as school was concerned, he was a total nobody. "You could do that, couldn't you?" he asked her hopefully. "Give me a hot girlfriend?"

She took the pipe stem out of her mouth. "No."

"Doesn't seem like it would be so hard," he grumbled.

Returning the pipe to her mouth, she leaned back in her creaking chair and puffed, eyeing him up and down like he was a marked-down day-old muffin. "Well," she said at last, "maybe I help you. But you must earn it, understand?" She leaned forward. "If not, I eat you for dinner."

He rolled his eyes. "Yeah, I get it, you're a witch. Relax." Did she think he was a gullible little kid? "So what do you need me to do?" Sacrifice chickens? Collect eye of newt? He could do that.

"Start with washing those." She jabbed her pipe stem toward the tiny kitchen sink, crammed with dirty plates and cups.

"You want me to do your dishes?" He would have preferred the eye of newt.

She let out a series of puffs like a threatening volcano. "For start," she said.

The water in the sink was cold and oily. It sucked at his fingers as he reached in to pull the plug. The sink emptied with a chunky gurgle, and for a second the drain looked like a gobbling mouth.

There was orange dishwashing liquid, which he squirted all over everything while hot water filled up the sink. The crusted egg yolk was a pain to get off, especially with the limp, smelly rag; he had to scrub it with a rusted knot of steel wool. One of the tea-stained mugs had a wet cigar stump floating inside, which he fished out and threw away, nearly gagging at the slimy texture. When the dishes were all clean, he wiped them dry and put them away in the cupboards, guided by the old lady's barked orders and jabbing pipe stem.

"I need to go," he said, sucking down the last of his tepid pop. If he hadn't done at least some of his homework by the time Mom got home from work, she'd drag Dad away from the TV and Dad would yell, "Why the hell can't you do what your mother tells you? Doesn't she do enough for this family?" And then he'd feel like crap. "So you'll take care of Matty now, right?"

A laugh like a farting horn burst out of her mouth, along with her dentures, which flew onto the table and skittered across it, chattering at him.

He leapt the width of the trailer like a startled deer. *What the* hell?

The old lady laughed harder, wheezing and knuckling her eyes. Finally, she picked up the still-snapping dentures and shoved them back into her mouth.

He sagged against the wall. It was just a stupid prank, he told himself. *Crazy old bat.*

Still grinning, she said, "You think is so easy? Is just beginning. Come back tomorrow. I give you another task."

"Man, how long is this gonna take?" he whined.

"It will take as long as it takes." She narrowed her eyes at him. "You don't want to do it, go home. What do I care?"

The old hag had him by the 'nads and she knew it.

***

"Today, Sasha—"

"Don't call me that!"

"—you will do dusting."

Her velour track suit was blue today. She was sitting in her chair with her legs stuck out, resting her slippered feet on the sofa. He winced away from the sight of her scrawny, scaly ankles. "Dust!" she commanded, pointing her pipe stem at a yellow feather duster hanging behind the front door.

While she supervised from her chair, he wagged the duster across whatever surfaces he could find—counters, windowsills, shallow shelves displaying ugly decorative plates. Clouds of dust rose, making his nose itch. The little figurines were the worst—he had to flick and twirl the duster to get into all their bumps and grooves. "You got way too many knickknacks, you know that?" he said, picking up a ceramic gnome and mashing feathers into its red-cheeked, bearded face. The gnome sneezed. He put it carefully back on the shelf and finished dusting without saying another word.

After the dusting came the vacuuming. The vacuum cleaner—an old upright—had a mind of its own. It roared and spat dust as he wrestled it back and forth across the trailer. "Also under furniture!"

she shouted, so he had to shove things around like Tetris blocks to get at the dust bunnies underneath. By the time he'd finished, the back of his t-shirt was soaked in sweat.

"There, I'm done," he said at last, wiping his forehead. Beyond the windows, shadows stretched across the clearing. "Can you do the spell or whatever now?"

"Light first." She tossed him a book of matches.

He caught it this time, in both hands, and grudgingly helped light her pipe. Smoke curled around her tangled hair.

"This Kravchuk boy, he give you trouble today?"

He shrugged. "Yeah, what else is new?" After PE, in the locker room, Alex had been doing his usual Houdini act, trying to change clothes under his towel, when he'd heard Matty's voice call out, "Hey, loser! What're those, boobs?" Alex had pulled his shirt on as quickly as possible, but not before one of Matty's flunkies piped up, "Man-boobs!" The rest of them laughed and echoed him like a flock of brain-damaged parrots, and Alex had a sudden horrible vision of this becoming his nickname for the rest of his high school career.

He scowled at the old lady. "When are you gonna do your part, huh? Or is this just a scam to get your housework done for free?"

"Housework is never free," she said, blowing smoke in his direction. "Come back tomorrow. Is more work to do."

***

The old lady wasn't kidding about more work. On Tuesday she made Alex clean the outside of the trailer, standing on a wobbly stepladder and scrubbing till his arms ached. On Wednesday he had to wash the windows, inside and out, using crumpled newspapers and eye-stinging ammonia. Thursday was laundry day—industrial-strength bras and baggy panties with dangling elastic. He shuddered at the memory. The washing machine was a rumbling monster in the "back yard"—more like a wilderness—and he had to hang everything out to dry on the spiderweb-shaped clothesline with wooden clothespins that pinched his fingers while wet laundry slapped him in the face.

The whole thing was a total nightmare. Every time he finished his chores, she told him to come back tomorrow. He'd had to invent some friends so his parents wouldn't get suspicious.

"Is my spell ready yet?" he asked for the umpteenth time, climbing the front steps.

"Today," said the old lady, ignoring him, "you clear front yard."

With a long-suffering sigh, he banged out the trailer door and down the front steps. There were dead branches all over the place, fallen from the trees overhead. He got his phone and his earbuds out of his backpack so he could at least listen to music while he worked, then started dragging the branches off the front path and throwing them into the underbrush. They clawed and scraped at him, leaving long red scratches on his arms. Next he pulled up the worst of the weeds—tall, tenacious plants that burned his palms when he yanked on them—and threw them after the branches. A few ravens gathered to watch him work, trading deep, hollow squawks as if commenting on his performance. He got the feeling they weren't impressed.

He found a rusted rake leaning against the trailer and used it to scrape the front path clear of decomposing needles. As he cleared the debris, the pale stones lining the path became more noticeable. Smooth and round, they almost seemed to glow against the dark earth. Curious, he bent down to touch one. It was cool, but not as cold as he'd expected.

Yanking out his earbuds, he knelt on the ground, letting the rake fall to one side with a twang. After brushing aside some dirt, he could make out a thread-thin crack snaking across the surface of the stone. There was a horrifying familiarity about it. When he tapped the stone with a fingernail, it made a light, hollow sound. The afternoon sun had slid behind the tall firs, sinking the clearing into shadow, and his skin was chilled where his sweat-damp t-shirt stuck to his back. One of the ravens darted across the clearing with a rustle of wings.

He began scrabbling at the dirt around the stone, pushing his fingers into the earth, grabbing at the stone's smooth edges. His fingers sank into a hole, two holes, like a bowling ball. He yanked up, and it came free in a shower of dirt.

Two gaping, earth-caked sockets, a row of teeth, a broken hole for a nose.

He dropped the skull, gagging, and staggered to his feet, scraping his hand frantically against his jeans. White skulls wound up and down the path, vivid against the dark ground. He could feel them all watching him. His sneakers skidded against the dirt as he snagged his backpack by a strap and ran away as fast as his legs would carry him.

At the bottom of the trail, he jumped on his bike and pedaled frantically down the old logging road. He was never going back. Possessed dentures and sneezing figurines were one thing, but a mass grave in the front yard? He shivered. Yeah, no. What if he'd been doing chores for a serial killer? What if she'd meant for him to be her next victim?

The down side was that on Monday he'd have to face Matty knowing he was on his own. But really, what was the worst Matty could do to him? At least he'd still have his head afterwards.

***

"So you are back. What happened?"

Alex threw his backpack to the floor and dropped onto the sofa. "I stood up for myself," he said bitterly. His hair was still wet from being dunked in a toilet bowl, though his shirt had mostly dried. Burying his face in his hands, he said, "It was a total disaster." He'd barely landed one feeble punch before Matty'd had him in a headlock. "He was in a real shitty mood, just looking for someone to take it out on. How was I supposed to know they lost the game Saturday night?" *You're a loser, Rusnak*, Matty had snarled at him, *and you'll always be a loser!*

"I don't even care if you kill him," said Alex. "Add him to your skull collection, whatever."

"You think so?" asked the old lady, her eyes bright.

He eyed her sideways. "So, like…why *do* you have all those

skulls?"

"They are pretty, no?" She gave a raucous cackle and rocked back in her chair, all but slapping her knee.

"You are so weird. For real." He hesitated, then asked, "You're not actually going to eat me, are you?"

"Tsk! No, no. Not anymore. You are too useful. And funny!" She chuckled.

"Yeah, sure—laugh it up. But can you really help me? Seriously? Tell me the truth."

"Yes," she said, suddenly sober. "I solve this Kravchuk problem, I promise you."

His heart rose. "Really?"

"Yes, really. But first you brush hair."

He touched his own still-damp hair, confused.

"No." She shuffled into the tiny bathroom and returned with a big wooden-backed hairbrush and a painted wooden comb. "Here." She thrust them into his hands and sat herself in the chair, scooting it around so her back was toward him.

"You want me to brush your hair?"

"Yes. Is beauty day. Next you do nails." He couldn't tell if she was serious or not.

He ran the soft brush through her rat's-nest hair, carefully undoing the tangles as best he could. Whenever he pulled too hard, she smacked him with her knuckles and he said "Ow!" pointedly.

Turned out she had been serious about the nails, but she'd meant her *toe*nails. She had him fill a big pot with hot water so she could soak her bony feet. Her nails were crazy long, curled like claws and hard as hooves. *Don't hurl*, he told himself, *don't hurl*. He lifted one of her damp feet in his hand; it was small and delicate, the skin blueish and crinkled like paper, loose around the knobby bones. With his finger and thumb jammed into the loops of a tiny pair of scissors, he sawed away at her nails until they splintered and broke off. "Dude, your toenails are gnarly," he said.

"Maybe you paint them for me, hmm?"

He looked up at her, horrified. She wouldn't! She cackled back at him. *Sadistic old bat.*

When he was done, her nails were a bit uneven, but at least they were a human length now. She squinted down at them, spreading out her toes gruesomely. "Very good," she said, and gestured for him to put her slippers back on. "Now I am hungry. You cook dinner."

He frowned, looking around the tiny trailer. "Okay, but where's the microwave?"

"Tcha! Push buttons is not cooking!"

"Fine! Jeez." He found a box of mac and cheese in one of the cupboards. There was a stick of butter in the fridge, and also a package of hotdogs. He chopped up the franks while the pasta boiled. Mom would've complained that there weren't any vegetables—maybe he should make a salad? The only thing in the crisper was a brown stain. "You got any veggies?"

The old woman made a face like he'd asked her to clean out the septic tank. "What for?"

He smiled. "Yeah, let's skip the salad."

They ate out of mismatched bowls, sitting at the little table. "Good," said the old lady after her first bite. "Very good." She gobbled up two bowlfuls and licked bright orange sauce off her lips with an unsettlingly long tongue. "You have done well, Sasha. While you wash dishes, I will make spell."

He clutched the dirty bowls to his chest. "Really?"

"In three nights is full moon." She paused and looked him in the eye. "If you are sure you want to do it. Is no undoing, after."

"Yes! Yes, I want to!"

She disappeared behind the curtain that hid the bedroom, while he hurriedly washed the dishes. He had just finished toweling off his hands when she reemerged. She was holding something white in her hand: an egg. In her other hand was a sewing needle. "Give me your finger."

He held it out nervously and yelped "Ow!" when she pricked him. A drop of blood welled up.

"Now put on egg, there."

The moment he placed his bleeding finger on the tip of the egg, a blood-red film crept down the shell from top to bottom. Soon the whole egg was a solid bright red.

"Good," said the old woman. "For spell to work, you must do exactly what I say. Are you listening?"

"Yes," he whispered, his breath tight in his chest.

"On night of full moon, you eat egg. Eat whole thing! Then you bury shells in the ground. Understand?"

"Where do I bury them?"

"Where?" She eyed him like he was some kind of idiot. "Does not matter! Ground is ground!" She placed the egg in his hand and carefully folded his fingers around it. "Do exactly as I say. Then your problems are all gone."

***

Early morning sunlight poured into the clearing. Alex pounded up the path to the trailer and jumped the three front steps in a single bound. He yanked open the front door, leaving it swinging on its hinges. "Undo your stupid spell!" he shouted. "Turn me back!" The screen door wheezed shut behind him.

The old woman shuffled through the bedroom curtain and into the kitchen. "Eh?" she said, blinking sleepily. "Whash thish?"

"Look at what you did to me!" he yelled, gesturing frantically at the wrongness of his body. His boobs—*actual* boobs!—ached from running up the trail, where they'd bounced all over the damn place, and he felt weirdly bottom-heavy, like a goddamn Weeble. Worst of all, where normally there would be a familiar weight and sensation between his legs, there was nothing. It was all...inside. "Put. It. Back!"

The old witch didn't look sorry at all. She smiled widely, showing off pink-red gums. "Ha, ha! Ish good look for you!"

She was hardly understandable without her dentures, which were chattering in their glass on the counter, wedged between a snowglobe and a souvenir beer stein. He grabbed the glass and shoved it at her, nearly shaking with fury. "You never said the spell would make me a fucking girl! Turn me back right now!"

The old woman finished popping in her teeth and waved her hand carelessly, like "no big deal." She went to the samovar and filled a glass with steaming tea.

"This is not okay!" shouted Alex. "My parents think I'm a girl!" After the horror of waking up to his new body (for the first time in his life, he'd been appalled to see a pair of tits), he'd sidled into the kitchen, expecting shock and confusion. Instead, Dad had looked up from his breakfast with a gentle smile Alex hadn't seen since he was ten and said, "How'd ya sleep, kiddo?" Mom had said, "Oh, Alex honey, is that what you're wearing to school?" and brushed his unexpectedly long hair back from his face.

"I can't go to school like this!" he'd gasped.

Mom and Dad exchanged a look. "You look fine, sweetie," said Mom. "I had acne too at your age—it'll clear up soon, I promise."

"It's not—!" Alex choked on the impossibility of explaining. Grabbing his backpack and a piece of toast, he pushed out the door with a gruff "Later," fighting hard not to cry.

"It's probably a boy," he heard Dad say before the door latched shut.

In the trailer, Alex said, "Undo it right now!"

The old lady shrugged. "Is not possible this minute. Come back later."

"*What?*" He took a step toward her, feeling homicidal, but then he remembered the skulls outside. She watched him impassively. With a frustrated noise, he turned and slammed out the door.

***

He came back that afternoon, right after school. "Is this your stupid idea of a solution?" he said, kicking open the trailer door. "Turning us *both* into girls?"

The first thing he'd seen when he got to school was Matty's face: they'd locked eyes all the way down the long, crowded hall. "You!" Matty had shouted. And she'd run straight for him.

She—he—was still tall, kind of lanky, hardly any boobs. Long blond hair in a sloppy ponytail. And just as fast as ever. While Alex stood there gawping like an idiot, she nailed him right in the nose with her fist.

He reeled back, clutching his face, his glasses askew. The crowd fanned out around them. Someone shouted "Catfight!" Warm liquid pooled in his hands and he tasted metallic saltiness.

"What the fuck is going on?" Matty yelled, her voice rising to a shriek. She grabbed the front of his shirt and shook him until his glasses were almost falling off. "Tell me!"

Coach Campbell broke in with "That's enough, young lady!" and yanked Matty back by the neck of her long-sleeved t-shirt. To Alex he said, "You okay, there?" and handed him an actual cloth handkerchief to press against his bleeding nose. Alex didn't know what was more surprising: Campbell's unprecedented sympathy or the fact that he carried around a hanky like some Victorian gentleman.

There was no "Walk it off!" this time; instead, Coach hauled them both to the vice-principal's office.

Mr. Singh folded his long fingers together on top of his desk and stared down at the two of them where they sat squirming in hard plastic chairs. "Now, girls. Why don't you tell me what this is all about, hmm?"

Alex and Matty exchanged a glance over Coach's bloody handkerchief. What could they say?

"We have a zero-tolerance policy for violence at this school," said Mr. Singh. Alex nearly scoffed out loud.

"Nothing to say for yourselves?" said Mr. Singh. Matty was staring down at her sneakers, scowling. "Matilda?"

She shrugged, one-shouldered. "Dunno."

"Is this about a boy?"

They rolled their eyes in tandem.

"All right, then," Mr. Singh sighed. "Matilda, I want you to go see the counselor. And Alexandra, go to the nurse and have her take a look at your nose."

The nurse was unsympathetic. "Nothing broken, and the bleeding's stopped," she said. "Put some ice on it when you get home. You'll be fine."

So much for his hope of being sent home early. "But shouldn't I wait here for a bit, just in case?"

"In case of what? Off to class with you!"

"Wait!" he said desperately. "I've got, like, period problems."

The nurse opened a cupboard and took out a package of Advil and a crinkly pink-wrapped square. "Anything else?"

Unlike the school nurse, the witch at least had some sympathy—enough to wrap some ice cubes in a scratchy towel for him. He pressed it against his nose, which still throbbed. "The whole day was a shit-show," he said. "I nearly walked into the boys' bathroom twice by mistake, and a bunch of girls laughed at me. And in Chemistry, Mr. Boyarski kept staring at my tits." It had made Alex's skin crawl. He'd crossed his arms over his breasts, wishing his t-shirt was baggier. He should have worn a bra, he realized. It hadn't even occurred to him. That was probably why the girl next to him had hissed "Slut!" during warm-ups in PE.

Lowering his makeshift ice pack, he said wearily, "Look, let's just agree the spell was a mistake. Just turn me back now so I can pretend this day never happened."

The witch pursed her lips and cocked her head at him like a bird. "Spell is not done for a while yet, I think."

"What do you mean 'not done'? *Make* it done!"

"Once spell is started…" She spread her knobby hands. "Is nothing anyone can do."

He was suddenly on his feet. "No! This morning you said you

could stop it!"

"I never said this." She wagged a gnarled finger back and forth in admonishment. "Before spell, I told you is no going back." Her eyes twinkled, like she was *laughing* at him.

"Take off the spell!" he shouted, slamming his hands down on the fold-out table hard enough to make it judder. "Now, dammit! Give me my dick back! Or I'll—"

Before he could finish the thought, the trailer started swaying like they were having an earthquake. The lights flickered. He stumbled and pressed a hand against the wall for balance. Little tendrils of carpet wriggled against his fingers, then the whole wall shivered, shaking him off like a horse dislodging a fly.

The old woman sat in her chair, unperturbed, while the windows rattled. "Do not be stupid little boy and make threats to me." She flicked her fingers in his direction, saying, "Go home, Sasha," and he was out the door and down the steps before he knew it. The clearing was still, with no sign of an earthquake, but one of the trailer's windows was still rattling as he walked away down the path.

***

He didn't go back until Friday, after he'd had a chance to cool down. He was still mad, of course—furious, actually—but the witch was his only hope of getting changed back. The bruise across his nose was a spectacular mass of yellows and greens now. But the world had not, in fact, ended, though he almost wished it would. "This *sucks*," he said feelingly.

"Is not so bad," said the old woman, packing her pipe.

"Says you!"

"No one is punching you now, yes?" She tossed him a matchbook, which he caught in mid-air.

"No, but Stacey Minchev and her crew keep laughing at me and calling me a skank!" Yesterday they'd hung an old bra on his locker. He couldn't believe he'd ever wanted to date one of them.

Still, he thought, as he struck a match and held it over the old woman's pipe, Amanda Nguyen had complimented him in English class, which had been kind of nice.

It was after Mrs. Lichenko assigned him a part to read out loud in *The Tempest*. He actually liked Shakespeare—it reminded him of J. R. R. Tolkien—but he'd sunk down in his chair, dreading his turn. If he did it badly, the teacher would think he didn't give a crap; if he did it well, the rest of the class would snicker at him. But then it occurred to him, while Barry Fraser was butchering Prospero's lines, that nobody cared if girls were into that kind of stuff. Girls were supposed to like English—even poetry. And he was reading Ariel, which was cool, especially because he got to do the part where the sprite says,

Full fathom five thy father lies
Of his bones is coral made
Those are pearls that were his eyes
Nothing of him that doth fade
But doth suffer a sea change
Into something rich and strange

And when he was done, Amanda, who sat in front of him, turned around in her chair and whispered, "That was really good. You should join drama club."

"Oh, uh, thanks," he said. He liked Amanda—at least, he thought she was sort of pretty, and cool in a nerd-girl way—but everyone knew drama club was gay. Like, really gay. At least, it was for guys. It was okay for girls, though. "Yeah, maybe, I guess."

So maybe being a girl wasn't 100% unadulterated awful. He wasn't telling the witch that, though.

"And how is Kravchuk?" she said, puffing away.

Today had been the first time he'd seen Matty all week—she seemed to avoid him after their fight. Then today he'd cut through the playground on his way home after school and there she was,

143

playing basketball with some boys like everything was normal.

You couldn't tell if she was wearing a bra or not, Alex noticed enviously. He himself was wearing two tank tops under his baggy hoodie. It sort of worked—kept him from bouncing around too much anyway, and no way was he wearing a bra. Below Matty's board shorts, her long, skinny calves were dusted with faint gold hairs. They hardly even showed. It was so unfair. Stacey had howled with laughter in the locker room at the sight of Alex's unshaven armpits. He wouldn't be caught dead in a pair of shorts.

Matty noticed him watching. Before Alex could slink away, she'd called a time out and was sauntering over to him, idly bouncing the ball. He braced himself.

"Hey," she said. *Bounce, bounce.* "Sorry about your nose."

He squinted up at her. Was this a trick?

"So what's the deal with this?" She waved a hand between them, balancing the ball lightly on her other hand. "Did you have something to do with it?"

He pressed his lips together tight enough to feel his braces, and shook his head. *Admit nothing*, he thought.

"Whatever," she said, shooting at the empty hoop behind him. She made it easily, of course. The ball came back and she bounced it a few times. "It's okay. I mean, I was pissed at first, but…" She shrugged. "It's not all that bad."

Alex gaped, forgetting to be scared. "How can you say that? This is literally the worst thing that's ever happened to me!"

"I dunno." She shrugged, eyes glued to the ball. *Bounce, bounce.* "My dad's way less of a hardass now. It's kinda nice, actually."

"Well…yeah, mine too," admitted Alex. "But what about your mom?" His kept wanting them to go clothes shopping together, a horrifying prospect.

"She doesn't live with us," said Matty.

"Oh."

"Hey, Matty!" shouted one of the boys. "We playing or what?"

Tossing Alex a careless "See ya," she jogged back to her game.

In answer to the witch's question, Alex said, "He seems to be rolling with it, I guess. I mean, he hasn't come after me again." A thought occurred to him. "But that doesn't mean everything is fixed! I'd rather be bullied than be a girl!"

"Now, now, Sasha," said the witch. "Spell will do what spell will do."

"Ugh. I hate you so much."

***

That weekend the last of the autumn heat finally broke with a night and morning of steady rain. By Monday afternoon it had turned into the kind of faint drizzle that Alex's mom called Scotch mist.

Alex ran up the trail, having left his bike at the logging road. The textbooks in his backpack thumped against his back. His sneakers splashed through puddles, and brush *thwapped* wetly against his jeans and shook raindrops down the neck of his rainjacket. Unable to keep the news to himself any longer, he shouted, "It wore off! I'm back, I'm okay! I'm a guy again!" His voice rang against the tree trunks.

The witch's clearing was empty.

A sliver of sunlight slipped through a split in the clouds, setting the raindrops on fire. It fell on low shrubs and a few stringy saplings: no trailer, no cinder blocks, no witch.

He stood there catching his breath, feeling lost. Maybe she was pissed at him. He had been kind of rude before. Had she left for good? Not that he cared, but… He pushed up his glasses and chewed on his lip. *Russian witch, lives in the woods, uses human bones for landscaping.* He wasn't stupid; he knew how to use Google.

He called out, "Baba Yaga!"

His voice dissipated between the dripping trees. From the top of a spruce, a raven launched itself across the clearing with a rattling croak and flapped off into the distance.

"Baba Yaga!" he shouted again. Water plopped from branches.

A third time, louder: "*Baba Yaga!*"

The echo of his voice faded.

A rustling came from the forest, faint and far away. He took a step forward, shoes squelching, and cocked his head. It was getting louder. It became a rushing sound, like a river in flood. Trunks creaked and branches snapped. Something was pushing its way through the woods—something big.

Thump! Thump!

His heart jumped into his throat. He took a step backwards and let his backpack fall to the ground.

A towering, whitish monster burst through the dark trees. Alex staggered, gaping up at it. It was the trailer, swaying back and forth on top of two giant chicken legs, like some kind of demented low-rent AT-AT.

It was simultaneously the weirdest and most terrifying thing he'd ever seen in his life.

The trailer-chicken waddled heavily into the clearing, shaking the earth with each step like a T. rex. It stopped, shuffled around to face him, and plopped to the ground, the cinder blocks falling into place from nowhere at the last minute. He could just see the huge chicken toenails (did chickens have toenails?) gleaming in the darkness underneath. Bits of damp branches and foliage stuck to the aluminum sides.

The front door began to rattle and shake. It flew open and the screen door slammed back. The witch stuck her head out. Her eyes were flashing and her hair stood up around her head in violent snarls. "Vy are you here?" she snapped.

He opened his mouth and blurted, "Do you want me to brush your hair?" He knew as soon as it left his mouth that it was a stupid thing to say, but her hair was seriously crazy, and after he'd got it so nice and smooth before.

The witch blinked. Then she threw back her head and gave her farting trumpet laugh, lips pulled back over long, sharp teeth. *No dentures today*, he thought a little giddily. "Sasha, you leetle monster," she said, smiling. "Come in."

Inside the trailer, the familiar pipe-smoke smell seeped out of the walls, where the carpet pile undulated like seaweed. When he sat down, after dropping his bag and his wet jacket on the floor, the sofa was warm underneath him. He could even feel a faint, deep *thud-thud,* like a heartbeat.

"So, you are boy again," said Baba Yaga, carrying her cup of tea to the table. "Congratulations."

"Thanks. Matty's still a girl, did you know?"

At school that morning, Matty had been surprised to see that Alex had changed back. "Sucks, dude," she'd said.

He'd blinked at her, pushing up his glasses. "You *like* being that way?"

Matty shrugged. She was leaning against the locker next to his, hands tucked into the pockets of her baggy jeans. "Yeah, didn't you? It's cool. Anyway, Dad says I don't have to be on the hockey team now if I don't want to, so it's all good."

Alex squinted up at her, trying to wrap his head around it. "So you're gonna, like, be a girl and date boys and stuff?"

"No! God! I'm still into girls, dumbass." She flicked his forehead with her middle finger.

"Ow." *Jerk.*

"You looked better before, you know. Oh, well. Later, loser," she said, smirking, and slouched off down the hall.

"Matty may be a girl now," Alex grumbled to the witch, "but she's still a dick."

The old woman chuckled, pulling out her pipe. "This Kravchuk makes a good choice."

"*Choice?* There was a choice?"

"Of course."

Alex mulled over her words as he reached for one of the matchbooks stacked on top of a purring ceramic kitten. After he'd lit her pipe, he said, "Well, if I did make a choice, I don't regret it for a second." He'd never been so happy to see his own body, in all its squishy, lumpy glory, as when he'd woken up that morning. His dick was back and in working order—he'd checked—and everything was where it should be. He'd never take his body for granted again.

On the kitchen counter, the dentures grinned and blew bubbles at him from inside their glass. A seashell figurine and a carved wooden bear waltzed back and forth across the countertop.

"So you're really Baba Yaga, just like in the stories? How come you're not in Russia, or Ukraine or whatever? I mean, why come *here* of all places?"

She snorted. "I do not go to places, they come to me! I live in the middle, where all forests meet."

"Oh, wow, like kind of a space-warp thing?"

"Eh?"

"A singularity? You know, like a wormhole? That's so cool!"

"Go home, Sasha," said Baba Yaga. "You make me tired."

"Yeah, I gotta go anyway," he said, gathering his still-damp jacket and backpack. "The drama club's doing a thing later." At the door, he stopped, fiddling with the screen latch. "Uh, so does that mean if I come back you're gonna, like, be around?"

The old woman frowned her hairy eyebrows into a forbidding V. "I am very busy!"

"Yeah, I totally get that, but I was just thinking, you know, if you needed some help around the house or whatever..." He shrugged again, staring at something behind her head. "I could, like, give you a hand."

Her eyes scoured him suspiciously. Then she dropped her gaze to the table, clearing her throat and turning her mug in little circles. "Maybe you can come tomorrow," she said. Looking up, she shot him a sly, toothy smile. "Maybe this time you paint nails, eh?"

He snorted, trying to hide a grin. "Man, you really are evil!"

***

Rebecca A. Coates is a writer and editor whose work has been published in *skirt quarterly* and *emerge 15*. She blogs about grammar and writing (and UFOs and werewolves and mermaids) at *Grammarlandia.com*. A graduate of the Writer's Studio at Simon Fraser University, she lives in Vancouver because she loves trees and hates sun. Baba Yaga has long been her favorite witch.

TEETH
Jessamy Corob Cook

One

There are all sorts of grannies in the wood. Some get eaten by wolves and others eat wolves. You can tell which is which easily enough— just look at the teeth. Are they soft and paper-yellow and crumbling with years of rice pudding and jam? Or are they iron hard and, apart from a speckling of rust, well equipped to slice through hot, canine muscle and crunch through bone?

Well, you have your answer.

Oh, I know she's not a granny in the biological sense. But she grandparents, if nothing else, the forest.

"You're late," she tells me, as I stumble into the hut, my legs stiff from the night's riding.

I know I am. I felt the rush of mild air and glimpsed the white streak of Dawn galloping past me as I approached the hut. We aren't supposed to pass, you see. We shouldn't be in the same place at the same time. It's one of the rules.

I sink into a chair as the door of the hut creaks shut and the hut resumes its slow rotation, setting the china chattering. You get used to it after a while.

Baba Yaga is looking at me, expectantly. You'd think she'd know better by now, but every morning on my return she has that gleam in her eyes. There's an almost innocent optimism in her unfailing certainty that the impossible can be done.

She says, "Well?"

I say, "No."

I undo the white buttons of my black cloak and let it fall over the back of the rickety wooden chair. The fire is roaring, and the air in the hut is dense with smoke and sweat and the smell of half-munched mouse (the cat is mid-breakfast.)

Baba Yaga says, "not one?"

I say, "I've been riding all night. I'm hungry."

She sets a bowl of gruel before me. It sloshes onto the table as the hut judders and jolts around. I pick up the spoon and begin to eat. I have learned that Baba Yaga's cooking is best enjoyed at speed, without stopping to look or taste or consider the ingredients.

Baba Yaga has turned her back to me, stirring and stirring at the pot on the stove.

"You had my hopes up, Sister," she says. "Not like you to be late. I was sure there was a reason. I was sure it was because you had found something precious."

I don't answer that. I can't, because I did discover something precious. But it isn't something I can tell her about.

But I need to say something. To ask her what I've never dared to before. Because things are different now. Last night changed everything. It's time to speak.

But I can't. I keep my head bent over my bowl and say nothing.

I scrape my bowl clean, pass it to the disembodied washing-up hands (I've yet to learn what became of the rest of the body) and climb the narrow, creaking stairs to the attic.

It took me a long time to learn to sleep in a constantly moving house. It doesn't move in the way a carriage trundles along a smooth road. It bumps and jerks and rattles. But somehow I have grown used to it. This attic is mine, and although my feet and head knock against opposite walls when I lie down, it's my space and here I can be private.

I collapse onto my heap of straw. I changed the straw only yesterday, and it still smells of summer and youth. I wrap my black cloak around myself and close my eyes. I'm shaking, I realize.

I saw her. I saw her, and she was beautiful. She was perfect.

I push the thought from my mind.

I muse, as I often do, on the others. The White Dawn and the Red Day. Where do they go when it is not their turn to ride? Where do they sleep? It's not a big hut for us to be always avoiding each other. One of us is always out riding, but that means two must always be here. And I have never seen them. I don't know who they are. Where they come from.

And what did they do to end up in service to Baba Yaga?

Two

Because I was a coward—and because, if I'm honest, there has always been more of darkness than of light in me, even in those days—I left at night.

I didn't tell John I was going. I left him a note. It said: *When she is old enough to ask, tell her I'm sorry, and I love her.*

I only realized days later that I should probably have expressed those same sentiments to John also.

Too late. I knew even then that I might never see them again. Many people go in search of Baba Yaga, but only the innocent return. That ruled me out.

When I reached the meadow that separated our orchard from the wilds of the forest I allowed myself one last look back at the white house. Before I left I had lit a lamp and left it burning low on the windowsill of her bedroom, where she lay now, dreaming in her cot. I could see it from where I stood at the edge of the orchard, glowing gold through the trees. I gazed at the light for a long moment, and then I turned away and headed for the darkness.

And, after weeks of searching for her, in the end it was she who found me. In those days I was an indoor creature, soft and lumpy, incompatible with forest. Dress ripped, hair matted, mud-spattered and cross as a toddler at nap time, I'd lumbered, predictably, into a bear trap. Like the witch herself, it had iron teeth. The teeth squelched into my podgy calf and I howled all afternoon. And then there she was. As if she could smell my blood. And she looked so changed from when I'd seen her last, and yet I knew her at once.

She must have known me too because she said, "Sister. What a delightful surprise."

I could only whimper. I thought she would leave me there, but she crouched beside me and gnawed through the trap as though it were a tough-ish parsnip. She picked me up and slung me into her outsized mortar—somehow, she had grown strong—and she paddled us away through the forest with the pestle. The seemingly unwieldy vehicle reached an impressive speed, crunching and bumping over bracken and roots, while briars and branches and even whole trees, shifted before us to make way for our thunderous approach. I was rattled about like a bean in a bowl.

By the time we reached the hut I was bashed and bruised and breathless. I barely noticed the fence of bones and skulls and the unnaturally large (not to mention hyperactive) chicken's legs which the hut was balanced on. I limped after her into the kitchen, where she brewed a swampy-smelling potion, and I sat and reassembled my senses as well as one can in a hut that won't stay still.

I said, "How did you find me, Angelica?"

"A little bird told me."

She spoke in a sing song, teasing voice. I have since learned that she was not being metaphorical—birds bloody love her. They'll tell her anything, the birds. Do anything for her.

She took the pot from the stove, dipped a rag into the steaming sludge and began to dab my wound with it.

"Sit still, Sister," she said, still in that disconcerting sing song way.

"Why do you call me Sister? We were stepsisters."

"Sisters is sisters. It's not about blood, is it? It's about that sisterly love."

I couldn't tell if she was teasing me or not.

"I don't deserve your kindness," I said.

She didn't disagree.

"I've come to say I'm sorry, Angelica," I said.

"That is not my name anymore, Sister. It was an entirely unsuitable name for me."

She began to bandage my leg. The bandages were grayish and smelled as though they'd last been used for washing the dog. The fingers which wound the bandages round and round were bony and hardened with forest living. So was her face. She was young then, still. Comparatively. And yet she was old.

And, of course, there were the teeth.

"I'm sorry," I said again. "And I want you to come and live with us. Come home with me. You can't live in this hut. It's filthy. And it's ridiculous. It won't stand still. You couldn't pick your nose in this place without the risk of poking out an eye."

"Fortunately, Sister," she said, knotting the bandage tight, "I have given up picking my nose."

"Well, it's no way to live," I said.

She stood and crossed the room, knelt to put a log on the stove, her back to me.

"Please," I said. "I am sorry for what I did. I truly am. Come home with me. You will have a comfortable bed and good food, and you won't be alone anymore."

"The forest is my home. I belong here."

"I wish you would let me help you. I want to make up for what I did. I'll do anything."

She turned to face me then. She grinned. Those teeth. Those iron teeth.

I shuddered.

She said, "Anything?"

Three

Baba Yaga's custom is to wake me as evening approaches by banging a broom handle on the ceiling below my attic. I knock on the floor to let her know I'm awake. I sit up. Brush away the memories that have clustered during the day's sleeping.

This is my life now and has been for many years. Every evening the same. And yet, even before my eyes are open, I know that something has changed. And then I'm swamped by the memory of last night and my skin shivers.

I saw her. I can see her again tonight.

I clatter down the stairs and out into the yard to wash in the frost-crisp water butt. The light is already fading. I find it odd these days to see daylight at all. A purplish dusk is the most I get. But my ability to see in the dark has developed to an extraordinary degree.

The hut is being obstinate this evening; it won't stop for me to climb back aboard, so I have to take a running leap next time the door is pointed in my direction. I've gathered all number of bruises in this way, but today I make it inside with little incident.

Baba Yaga's at the stove when I enter the kitchen. Through the thin wall I hear the click-clack of the loom in Baba Yaga's room. So, there was a new arrival today.

"Another child, Baba?"

She says, "They always seem to find me. It's uncanny."

She puts a bowl of stew on the table and hands me a tin spoon. I pick up the spoon and put it down again. Look at her. Take a breath.

"Baba. Listen. I am not young anymore."

"Neither of us are young anymore, Sister."

She grins at me. She knows I hate to see the teeth.

155

"I've searched, Baba Yaga, everywhere. For years I have searched, night after night. Every inch of the forest. I have climbed every tree and swum every river and dug my way through mud and bracken and bramble. They can't be found. It's impossible—"

She cuts me off with one raised finger. Over her shoulder she calls out, "I can't hear any clickety-clack, girly!"

The sound of the loom, which I didn't notice had stopped, resumes.

Baba Yaga turns back to me, and there's a fire in her eyes I know only too well. But I can't give up now.

"You see what I'm saying. I've done everything I can. I've served my penance, and now you must let me go."

The lips curl back. The teeth clash and clatter. It's deafening. The hut shakes and outside the wind begins to roar.

"We had a deal! We had a deal!"

She's screeching. With every word the teeth clang. Lightning flashes across the evening sky beyond the window.

I shrink into my chair.

"YOU GAVE ME YOUR WORD, *SISTER!*"

And the sky cracks with thunder.

Her breath hisses though her iron teeth. "It's your time to ride. Now get out and do what you agreed to do. You will not leave here until your task is complete."

I pull on my black cloak. Fumble with the buttons. I pull my hood up as I head outside. The storm is still raging, and rain is splashing down like pebbles.

At least Baba Yaga's rage has left her no room for suspicion. No room for her to wonder just exactly why, after all this time, I am asking for freedom tonight.

Four

My closest companion now is Never. (My horse. Not my choice of name.) After years of riding out together night after night it's difficult not to become attached. The bounce of the saddle beneath me and the thudding of her hooves on the forest floor are an extension of my own heartbeat. I spend my days being jolted every which way by that house—Never's rhythmic, steady movement feels like stillness by comparison.

Never and I did not take to each other straight away. When Baba Yaga lead Never from the stable on my first night I could only gasp.

"But…she's enormous!"

"Isn't she?" Baba Yaga patted Never's neck, proud.

"I can't ride her."

I'd learned to ride on Breeze, a sweet natured pony who'd take me a few laps of the meadow on mild afternoons when I was a child. As Baba Yaga knew perfectly well. I hadn't ridden since I'd married.

"We made a deal," Baba Yaga said. "You know what you have to do. You will be my Black Midnight. It's an honor, really. Of the three, everyone knows you're the best. I'm giving the honor to you. Only because you're my sister, Sister."

She gave me my cloak. Long, woolen and, thankfully, warm. I pulled it around my shoulders. It had a row of little white buttons in the front. I fastened it up to my chin.

"All night?"

"All night. Every night. But I'm a reasonable person, you know, sister. So it won't be forever. As long as you do something for me."

"Anything."

"Bring me back my teeth. Every lovely, little white one. When you have found them all, then all will be forgiven, and I will let you go."

I gaped at her. I opened my mouth to tell her that it's impossible, that those tiny teeth could be scattered across the world by now. But I didn't say that.

I said, "You don't have a smaller horse?"

She laughed.

And so I had to learn to ride through the forest on this dark, muscular giant. Never had no patience for timidity, and if she sensed any in me she would shake me off like a dog shakes off droplets of pond. And in this way she taught me to be bold.

Five

It was nearly three years after joining Baba Yaga, and riding out night after night, before I went back to the white house. This was partly because the pain was too new, and I didn't want to see what I couldn't have, and partly because in those days I was devoting myself, like a good little witch's servant, entirely to my task. But three years of slithering through undergrowth and scrambling up trees and not a single tooth to show for it had worn away at every feeling but longing.

To see her. A glimpse through a window. Just to see that she was happy.

That night when I rode out I guided Never through the trees towards the one place I had always avoided: home. I dismounted at the edge of the orchard. It was spring, and the moon lit the apple blossom and painted the trees silver. I left Never to graze in the meadow, and made my way through the orchard, my heart hammering out questions: what exactly was the size and shape of a three-year-old? Would she be buried beneath her blanket or did she still sleep, as she used to, with her face towards the window? Would I see dreams in her face? Had John found a new wife since I'd gone? A new mother for her? Would New Mother be there, by the bed, singing to my baby as I used to sing to her?

The house was dark. No lamp in the window tonight. But the moon was bright, and anyway my eyes had had three years of night-looking to practice in by then. In the old lifetime we had a ladder that John and I used to reach the higher apples in the orchard during picking time. It used to be kept behind the stable. I went to look, and it was still there. And if I'd had my wits about me then I would have noticed that the stable was full of silence. There was no stamping of hooves, no snort of horse-breath. There was no smell of fresh manure in the air, only a damp, clinging scent of rotting straw. But I didn't notice.

The ladder didn't reach her window, but it got me high enough to cling by my fingertips to the window ledge and, kicking with my feet against the wall beneath, I pushed myself up onto it. Three years of climbing trees not entirely wasted.

The window was boarded up.

I slithered my feet back down the wall, hands still gripping the window ledge, till my toes found the top rung of the ladder, and I climbed back down. I saw now what should have been obvious from the start, clear as day in the icy light of the moon: every window was boarded up. I circled the house to be sure, but I knew already what I would find. It was the same on every side.

Along the path that lead up to the front door there ran a mossy garden wall. I ran my hand along it and felt the wobble of the loose stone. I prised it out, my fingers tingling with the familiarity. Yes, the spare key was there.

I ran up to the door. The key scraped in the lock, a screech of rust unexpectedly disturbed, but it turned. I pushed open the door. I tried to step through it but couldn't. Some invisible barrier was in my way—Baba Yaga's magic keeping me out of my old world. But in the slice of moonlight I'd let through the door, I could see clearly enough into the hallway and the rooms beyond. The furniture was draped with sheets. The floor was fuzzy with dust. Everything was still. Nobody had been here for a long time.

They were gone.

Six

Because she knows me, Never knows that I want to follow the same path we followed last night. It's a long way, but the nights are lengthening now, and I have time. We outride Baba Yaga's storm, though my cloak is still heavy with rain. As I ride the night wind dries it somewhat. At last we reach the edge of the forest and emerge into starlight. I dismount and set Never to graze in the meadow. I don't tether her—I know she'll be there when I return.

I approach the white house through the orchard. And, of course, it might all have been a dream. Yesterday might not have been real. I might reach the house to find every window dark, just as they have been dark for all these past years.

But then I see it: a gleam of gold. On the ground floor, at the far corner of the house, in what used to be my drawing room, and now is hers. A lantern in the window.

It was real.

I crouch by the lighted window. My heart flutters. I peer into the warm glow of the room.

She's there.

She's a woman now. And on her knee is a baby. She's singing to the baby.

I knew her the moment I looked through the window last night, but if I hadn't known her by her face I would have known her by the song. The song I used to sing to her. The song my own mother used to sing to me. I have to press my ear up against the glass to hear it.

Fly, fly away into the night,
Fly little black bird until it is light,
Fly as far as you will, for I know, though you're gone,
The treasure you seek it was here all along,
Fly little bird, and while we're apart,
When your treasure is lost, simply look to your heart.

I lean, heavy, against the window and let the singing warm my bones. After she has fallen asleep in her chair, the bundle of baby lolling in her lap, I gaze through the glass, drinking it in.

A man enters the room. For a moment he watches, like me, an observer of this perfect scene of which he is not a part. We won't—can't—intrude. Or, at least, I can't. He steps across the carpet. Crouches by the chair. Kisses the baby's forehead. Then lays a hand on my daughter's shoulder. She stirs and smiles. Passes him the baby, who slouches, heavy, on his chest.

She turns and begins to approach the window, and for a moment my heart is ice and my breath freezes, but I realize she's only going for the lantern. She can't see me. Even if I were stood before her very eyes, there in the lighted room, she wouldn't see me. I'm not in her world.

They leave together. I see the light from the lantern gleam briefly from the window of the nursery upstairs, and then it's dark. I stay by the window of the drawing room and stare at the fire in the hearth, until it has burned low and I am heavy with dew and longing.

Evangeline. That was the name I gave her.

I realize I've named the baby without meaning to. In my mind she's called Isabella. She looks like an Isabella.

The cold of the night washes over me. I don't want to go. But I'm running out of time. I must be back at the hut by morning.

I drag myself to my feet. My joints crack and creak.

I did it for her, I remind myself. When I left, it was for Evangeline. When I swore service to Baba Yaga, it was for Evangeline. It was all for her.

Seven

I'm late again. I pass Dawn on my way to the hut, as she rides out. We don't speak. Her cloak is white, as mine is black. She doesn't look at me.

I lead Never to the stable, scrape the stones from her hooves, give her an armful of hay.

I'm tired.

"You're late, Sister," she says when I enter the hut.

She has a crow perched on her arm. Their heads are together. Obviously they are mid-chat. Birds always take priority, so I sit and wait. As I fumble with the little white buttons on my cloak I watch the child. The same one from last night, I assume. She's crouched on the floor, sorting grains of rice. She gives me the briefest of mistrustful glances, her eyes, too big for her little face, surly. But she won't be deterred from her task, and she bows her head once more.

The crow flaps out through the open window. Iron teeth scrape and clatter as Baba Yaga turns her attention to me.

"Did you find anything last night, Sister? Anything precious?"

That look again. Every morning. Like she really believes that today she'll get a different answer.

I shake my head.

She sets a bowl in front of me, and I eat as the sky lightens beyond the window. I watch the child sort the rice. I've developed a sudden affection for little girls. With every jolt and jerk of the hut the grains roll, muddling themselves, good and bad, just as before. She continues anyway, dogged, focused. The threat of becoming dinner can have that effect. But the task is all but impossible. You would think she would despair, but she doesn't.

I look to Baba Yaga. She's been watching me watching the girl.

I say, "I have a daughter."

She says, "I know."

I say, "And she has a child too. Will you not let me visit them? One night. Just one night in the human world. Then I'm yours."

I'm prepared for more screaming and storms. But she sits at the table beside me. Bares her teeth. The gums and the soft flesh of her mouth are scraped raw. "If you want to leave, Sister, you know what you must do. When your task is complete I will let you go."

"One night?"

"No."

"But why? I know what I did was terrible, but you've punished me enough. Why do you keep me here? What good am I to you? Why don't you find someone else to be your Black Night?"

She turns away from me, watching the child, who's pretending not be listening.

I stand to go upstairs. Her voice stops me.

She says, "You came here of your own free will, Sister. I offered you a deal and you agreed. All of this you have brought upon yourself. All these years you could have been living in that big house with your pretty family, happy ever after. But you came to me."

I go upstairs. I sink on to my straw bed. I close my eyes and listen to the morning birds singing.

Eight

"Doesn't it worry you?" Mary asked over the squirming head of her round, blond one-year-old. "I mean, living out here on the edge of town, with that great, dark wood looking over your shoulder?"

I said, "Woods don't look."

The other child, a chubby, pink-faced little girl, was slouched next to her mother. She was swinging her legs, knocking her shoes against the velvet of the sofa. As I watched I felt a kick back inside me, as if the baby could see through me, and wanted to join in. I stroked a hand over my bulging belly.

"But you'll have a family soon," said Mary. "It isn't safe all the way out here. All sorts of unsavory characters hide in those woods. Criminals. Gypsies. Not to mention the wolves and bears."

The lumpy baby on her lap was tugging at the front of Mary's dress, and she obligingly unbuttoned. He latched himself onto the nipple. His sister watched with unconcealed envy.

"Maybe you aren't worried now," Mary went on, "but it will all be different when the baby comes. You'll see. Becoming a mother changes everything. Children do get lost in those woods, you know. It happens. They wander off the path and can't find their way home."

I nodded and let her lecture on, because I couldn't be bothered to argue. After a while an unholy stench began to issue from the baby, and Mary bustled off to change him, leaving me and the older sister in gruff silence.

We stared at one another. She began to swing her legs again.

"Please don't kick the sofa," I snapped.

Her legs grew still. She glowered.

I found her alarming. When I thought about how my own baby would be I always imagined her tiny, delicate and permanently giggling. Or asleep. Nothing like this.

"There's a witch in the woods," the girl said, suddenly.

She had decided to continue with her mother's theme, apparently.

I said, "No, there isn't."

"There is."

"Your mama tells you those things to scare you. To stop you running off. There aren't any witches. And I asked you *not* to kick the sofa."

She sulked for the rest of the afternoon.

Then, when the installation of the writhing baby into the perambulator was complete, and they were halfway out the door, the girl turned, tugging at her mother's hand.

She said, "There is a witch in the woods, so there."

"Come along, Arabella," said Mary.

But the kid planted her stocky form in my doorway and wouldn't budge. "I've seen her. She eats children. I know, because of her teeth."

Mary said, "Arabella!"

I said, "Teeth?" and for a moment my heart seemed to stop.

"Yes. Her teeth are all pointy, like a wolf. And they aren't made of tooth."

Mary began to drag the child away along the path.

I called after, "What are they made of?"

They were nearly out of sight now. But I heard, without any

doubt, the shrill little voice calling back to me.

"They're made of metal!"

Nine

I wake, as always, to the bang of the broom handle. Dreams of years ago cling to me like brambles. I shake them off.

She's too busy chatting with a bunch of starlings at the window to notice me enter the kitchen, so I help myself to stew from the pot, and sit at the table to eat.

The girl must have finished sorting the rice, because she's sat in the corner, back to the wall, legs splayed out and she's separating needles from pins. She seems to have befriended the cat, who has draped himself across her shoulders. A good thing for her—the ones who get on with the animals usually seem to survive.

The sparrows flutter away. Baba Yaga picks up a log too large for the stove, and gnaws it in half before shoving it in. She claws out splinters from her mouth, and her fingernails scrape against iron. I shudder, but the child takes it in her stride, and hums as she continues her sorting.

Outside the shadows are growing long, sunset blood seeping into the sky.

"Time for you to go, Sister," Baba Yaga says, bright and breezy.

Our conversation the night before might never have happened.

I say, "We aren't sisters. We were never sisters. I wish you would stop calling me that."

"But we are," she says, and she gives me another steely flash of those teeth. "You and me, me and you—we're two sides of the same coin, *Sister*. Like it or not, we're sisters in every way that matters."

I'm too outraged to answer this. I pull on my cloak, and stamp towards the door, muttering to myself.

I have never heard such nonsense.

The hut wobbles as I reach the door, and I tumble down the steps, and end up tangled in my own cloak, which doesn't help my mood at all.

Never always calms me: her smell, as I open the stable door. The white horse gives an indifferent snort as I enter. She knows it's not her turn. The brown horse is still out riding—I only see her in the mornings.

I saddle Never, stroking my hand along her warm, rough back.

I whisper to her, "I don't know what to do."

I ride out into the woods. I should go and look for teeth, but what's the point? I've searched every inch of the forest, from the top of the highest tree to deep within the earth. I've waded through the rivers and even crept into the dens of wolves, blazing torch in hand, sweating through the stench of blood. The creatures snarled and snapped at me, and sometimes tried to guzzle a limb or two—I always keep a knife at my belt, and somehow have so far come out alive. But searching a forest for a few teeth is madness. I might search for a thousand years and not find one.

Never knows my mind before I've made it up myself. She carries me once more to the edge of the orchard. And so I spend another night outside the white house, crouched at the window, watching.

Ten

Babies do change your perspective somewhat. My theory is it's the size. When something that small becomes your world, your world must shrink. And the things you had the space to ignore are suddenly digging into your ribs.

My baby was very small. She arrived purple and squashy, like a skinned rabbit, and not much bigger. Her eyes, though, were floating hazelnuts, and mesmerizing. Within a few weeks she'd smoothed out into a cherub, rosebud pink, creamy. Her hair, like her Daddy's, was golden.

Evangeline.

Every mother thinks her baby is perfect, so I won't go on about it.

She was born in the spring, and I would take her out into the orchard behind the big, white house, where it was warm and smelled of grass. I would sit with my back resting against my favorite apple tree, and Evangeline in my lap. I sang to her, as the blossom drifted over us like snow. Sometimes John would join us. I taught him every song I knew, just in case—though I didn't tell him this—there came a time when I couldn't sing to Evangeline any more. But I liked it best when it was just the two of us, me and my baby, in a world where the sky was always blue and the sun never set and the supply of apple blossom was endless.

And yet.

The more perfect was Evangeline, the more dark and ugly I perceived myself to be. Guilt lurked like a shadow in the back of my mind, and my baby was the light that cast the shadow. It was for Evangeline that guilt itched at my insides, because I was the stain on her perfection. This pretty little blob was innocent, and I was not. It was wrong that I should be the one to sit with her beneath the apple blossom. It was wrong that I should be the one to sing her to sleep. I was poison to her.

All this I pushed to the back of my mind, but guilt is a hungry creature which will nibble insatiably. I'll corrupt her, I thought. How can I bring her up to do right, to be good, when I am rotten inside?

But for all that, I couldn't leave her. How could I leave her? She was mine.

Eleven

I like to think it's because, somehow, she knows I'm there, or senses I'm there—somehow she feels drawn to me—that she stays so long by the drawing room fire. After, long after she's put the baby to bed, she's still there. She came back downstairs, hours ago. For a while she read her book, but now it lies still in her lap, and she simply gazes into the fire. And every so often—I swear to it—her eyes wander over to the window where I'm crouching, pressed against the cold glass. As if she can see me. And those hazelnut eyes are perfect, and fill up my insides with warmth, even though the nights are turning wintry, and there's a bite of frost in the air.

It shoots through me like a bolt of lightning when I look up and see the sky to the east is streaked with gray. It can't be dawn. I've only been here the length of a sigh. But it's unmistakable. Day is on the way.

I leap to my feet and start to run, my steps crunching the frozen grass, through the orchard. Never is waiting, impatient, and I jump up into the saddle and dig my heels in, sharp. She doesn't need telling twice. We thunder through the forest. Branches catch on my cloak, tear at my hair, scratch my face, but still I urge Never forward, faster, faster, as all the while a watery lemon light is beginning to spread across the horizon.

Never picks up on my frantic energy. She's all over the place. She knows this forest better than I do, and I've never known her to be less than entirely sure-footed, but now her hooves are skidding and sliding in the mud. Then her leg catches on a tree root, she stumbles, and I am sent flying over her head.

I thud onto the ground. My breath is knocked out of me. Never is whinnying wildly. For a moment pain surges through me and I can't move. But it starts to subside, and I climb carefully to my feet. Test out my body, cautiously. Nothing broken. Only bruised.

I look up in time to see a wave of crimson wash the sky, and then the vast, circular edge of a smoldering winter sun breaks over the horizon. I wince as it reaches my night owl eyes, and look down.

I'm too late. I've broken the rules. Now she'll never let me go.

Twelve

Spring had turned to summer. I woke to the sound of her wailing. It was barely light, but the night had been hot and the morning was already beginning to simmer. The sun always reaches her window first. It must be shining on her cot, baking her. I should move her to a cooler room, at the back of the house.

John was stirring beside me. He heard Evangeline crying with no more or less interest than he heard the doves in the tree outside the window. He grunted as I slipped out of the bed, rolled over and opened one eye.

"Let her cry. You'll spoil her if you go clucking like a mother hen every time she whinges."

I left the room. Sometimes John made me seethe, and it was all I could do to keep my anger from exploding. Why should he criticize me for acting like a mother? When, after all, that's what I was?

The curtains were drawn across her window, but they were flimsy, and the sun was singing through them. I bent over her cot. Her eyes were scrunched, her tiny hands clenched and her red mouth spread wide as she roared.

Then I saw it. Nestled in the pink gum, just poking through, like a new shoot in spring.

A tiny, white tooth.

That was the moment I knew I had to leave.

Thirteen

We approach each other along the path, still a good half mile off from the hut. In the light of what is undeniably dawn, I see her face clearly for the first time. She's young. Not much older, probably, than my daughter. She can't have been doing this long. Or perhaps something about being the Dawn keeps her young in the same way as I was old within only a few weeks of being Night. After countless years I am ancient.

As we draw closer I call out, "Greetings!"

I'm already out after sunrise, so what does it matter if I break another rule?

I think she isn't going to stop, but then she does. Our horses bump noses in greeting. They are old friends who share a stable, even if their riders have never met.

She doesn't meet my gaze. Her expression is full of uncertainty. We don't break rules. Or, we never have before.

She says, "Why are you out when it isn't your time? Have you been given special permission?"

Her voice is even younger than her face.

I say, "Yes."

"Oh!" Her face clears. "And you have permission to speak to me?"

"Yes. Only for today."

She nods, earnestly. She still won't look into my eyes, but keeps her gaze at a point just below my chin. She seems to be lost in thought. After a moment she looks away.

She says, "Have you come to give me advice?"

"Advice?"

"Yes. I've been White for almost a year now, but I know I'm ready to become Red. But, of course, I can't be promoted until I've counted every leaf in the forest. I'm sure there's a way to do it, probably a really simple way, if I could only see it. But you must have done it when you were White. Perhaps you could just give me a small hint?"

"I don't understand. I was never White."

"But how did you become Black?"

"I… It just happened."

She frowns. She's looking at that same spot again—just below my chin. "She made you Black right away? I thought you had to earn it. Work your way up."

"Earn it? It's not a reward, girl. It's a punishment."

Her eyes flicker, briefly, up to meet mine at last. Then down again. She's confused.

She says, "I must go."

I pull Never over to the side of the path to let her pass. She begins to move off, then hesitates.

"A punishment for what?"

She really is very young. Barely more than a child.

I say, "Something unforgivable."

She canters away through the trees. And, because I'm late anyway, I stay there, listening, until the sound of the white horse's hoof beats have faded away.

Fourteen

There are all sorts of wicked older stepsisters. Some get their eyes pecked out and others peck out eyes.

Well, alright, it wasn't her eyes. As you know, it wasn't her eyes.

Angelica, as was her name in those days, was the prettiest little downtrodden stepsister you ever did see. My mother dressed her in rags and sent her to work in the kitchen, so she was always grease spattered and smudged with ash, but it made no difference—her beauty shone through grease and grime. And there was that smile—a perfect bouquet of little snow-white teeth. I could never hope to compete.

And so, when a rich young man with golden hair moved into the big, white house at the edge of the town and I felt my mother start to scheme, I was afraid. I didn't want to let my mother down. It's not that I'm making excuses, you understand. I should have known better.

The young man paid us a visit. He told us he was having a party in the big white house and we were all invited. And his eyes lingered on the beautiful kitchen girl. And the beautiful kitchen girl smiled.

After he'd gone my mother and I exchanged a long look. And then I went down to the kitchen. She was on the stone floor, scrubbing and singing, and she didn't hear me coming. I picked up a frying pan. Stepped towards her. My shadow fell across her face. She leaped to her feet, turned to me, eyes wide, mouth in a startled little gape, teeth gleaming white.

You've guessed the next bit, haven't you? Well, I'm going to say it anyway: I smashed the frying pan into her pretty little mouth. I smashed it again and again, until every perfect, pearly tooth had gone rattling across the kitchen floor and blood dripped down her chin.

I gathered the teeth into my cupped hands. I didn't look at her. I went out into the garden and flung the teeth as high as I could, and birds at once came flocking—crows and ravens, doves and pigeons, sparrows and robins—and snapped up the teeth in their beaks and carried them away in all directions, never to be seen again.

And I married the young man with the golden hair.

Fifteen

I'm expecting thunder, lightning, hurricanes. But she just glowers at me.

"Late again, Sister."

I gape at her. "Is that it? You're not going to munch my bones? You're not going to curse me? Turn me into a worm and feed me to one of your bird friends?"

"I don't need to, Sister. I know you won't be so foolish again."

I don't know what to say. She sets a bowl of gruel on the table, as though this were any other morning.

Which, apparently, it is.

I sit and begin to eat.

The girl is struggling with the needles and pins. The neat little piles scatter and merge with every jolt of the hut, and, of course, Baba Yaga won't give her bowls to put them in. Poor kid.

"I must warn you, though, Sister," Baba Yaga tells me, as she chops hemlock roots, "if you ever speak to one of the other riders again, I'll bite off your pretty little fingers."

My heart sinks. Of course she knows. Her bloody little feathered spies.

"A little bird told me," she says, as if I hadn't already guessed.

I watch her chopping. She hasn't asked me yet if I found anything last night. She's forgotten. And then I realize—she already knows. She always knew I would never succeed. She set me an impossible task to keep me here forever. That hopeful look she gives me every morning is all part of her deceit. She tricked me.

The heat of the fire is suddenly overwhelming. I reach for the buttons of my cloak. Then I notice the girl. She's paused in her work, a bright needle (or pin, who can tell?) gleaming between her fingers. She staring at me. Or, rather, she's staring at my buttons.

When she sees me looking she quickly looks away. I unfasten my cloak and shrug it off. I finish my gruel. Pass the bowl over the ever-ready floating hands. I go upstairs.

Sixteen

This day there are no dreams. No nagging memories. Just the dusty beams of sunlight pouring through the cracks in the roof of my attic. Just the dry smell of straw, three days old. Just the scrabble of mice beneath the floorboards. Pigeons chanting and starlings chattering overhead.

My past is gone. The best I can do now is forget it.

Seventeen

"Where is she?"

Baba Yaga is at the table dissecting a lizard. "Where is who?"

She must know I mean the child.

She's occupied, so I help myself to stew from the pot on the stove. Eat quickly, although it's hot. Nights are drawing in, and it will be my time to ride out soon.

Then I drop my spoon suddenly. The child isn't here. That can mean only one of two things. I peer into my bowl at the suspicious something floating there.

Baba Yaga laughs (as always, toothily). "No little kiddies in the pot today, Sister. I wouldn't waste nice, juicy kiddy on you. No; I let the little pumpkin go."

"You let her go?"

"She completed her tasks. Say what you like about me, Sister, but I always keep my word."

"She finished sorting the needles and pins?"

Baba Yaga picks up a cloth from the corner of the room, unfolds it and holds it up for me to see. It's the child's apron. Down the left side is stuck neat little rows of silver pins, and down the right the same of needles. She found a way to keep them secure and stop them rolling off at the whims of the excitable hut. That was why, I suddenly realize, she was staring at my buttons. It must have given her the idea. I'm impressed. Simple, but clever.

"The thing about children," Baba Yaga says, "is they *believe* a thing can be done, and they do it. It's all about being able to see what's under your own nose."

"Or perhaps it's that the tasks you set the children actually can be done."

She says, "I don't set impossible tasks. I play fair."

Which is so patently untrue my blood begins to sizzle.

I push my bowl away. Child-meat or no child-meat, I've been sufficiently put off.

And she hums to herself as she massacres the remains of the lizard. It's a tune I know, and it makes my skin crawl. A tune she must have heard my mother sing to me. That I sang to my daughter. That my daughter now sings to her daughter.

I grit my teeth, grab my cloak and slip past Baba Yaga. When I reach the doorway the hut lurches—I'm sure it does it deliberately—and, as happens so often, I'm flung down the steps and thud onto the ground. I can hear her laughing, softly, inside. It's nothing short of white hot rage that brings the tears to my eyes. She's a liar. The task she set me is impossible. Those teeth could be scattered across the world by now. They can't be found. It can't be done. And now I'll spend the rest of my life, night after night, watching through a window.

From within the hut I hear Baba Yaga, not humming anymore but singing aloud.

Fly, fly away into the night,
Fly little black bird until it is light,
Fly as far as you will, for I know, though you're gone,
The treasure you seek it was here all along…

She's mocking me. I won't listen. I scramble to my feet, wiping my face with my hands, fling my black cloak over my shoulders and go to the stable to saddle Never, buttoning the little white buttons across my chest.

Eighteen

The mornings are getting colder. Any day now I'll wake up to snow. The thought thrills me.

The wind is in my hair, my white cloak rippling out behind me. Steam is already rising from Always' snowy back as we canter through the honey-gold sunrise forest. She's enjoying this as much as I am.

But there's an uneasiness in the back of my mind, like a shadow.

Since I spoke with Black Night I've begun to think, and think too much. At every dawn since that day, as I ride out, I've half-hoped, half-dreaded that I might meet her again.

I haven't. Not yet. But it plays on my mind. I thought all this was for a reason. I thought it was a trial. You begin as White, then if you pass the test you progress to Red and then to Black, and each time you learn a little more, understand a little better. That's what I thought. After Black, I thought, you became a witch in your own right, like Baba Yaga herself.

And that's what I want. That's why I'm doing this. To be like her.

But now I'm not sure if any of that is true. Or if we're all just pieces in some game Baba Yaga is playing.

She looked old, the Black Night. Old and sad.

And there was something deeply unsettling about those buttons. I could barely take my eyes off them. I can't stop thinking about them, even now.

Who would wear a cloak with buttons made of teeth?

***

Jessamy Corob Cook is an actress, writer and Londoner. She recently won first place in *Writing Magazine's* adult fairy tale competition and second place in *Caterpillar Magazine's* children's story competition.

ABOUT THE ANTHOLOGIST

Kate Wolford is a writer, editor, and blogger living in the Midwest. Fairy tales are her specialty. Previous books include *Beyond the Glass Slipper: Ten Neglected Fairy Tales to Fall in Love With*, *Krampusnacht: Twelve Nights of Krampus*, and *Frozen Fairy Tales*, all published by World Weaver Press. She was the founder of *Enchanted Conversation: A Fairy Tale Magazine*, at fairytalemagazine.com.

ACKNOWLEDGEMENTS

No book gets published without a lot of help, and this book is no different. Thanks to Sarena Ulibarri, Editor-In-Chief of World Weaver Press, who stepped in to finish the editing of *Skull and Pestle: New Tales of Baba Yaga*, when life got in the way of my doing so. And another big thank you to Amanda Bergloff, Editor-in-Chief of *Enchanted Conversation Magazine*, who wrote the delightful introduction to this book.

Enchanted Conversation's existence is why every book I've anthologized exists. The success of EC, when I was publisher (and am now founder), got my foot in the door at World Weaver Press, and for that I will always be grateful.

But I'd like to give special thanks to the people who've supported EC over the years, and most particularly those who donated money to the Enchanted Conversation Fundrazr campaign of 2017. Every penny went to keeping the magazine alive.

Extra special thanks go to the top donors. Some wished to remain anonymous, and I'll honor that, but to Judy DaPolito, Marcia Sherman, E. J. Hagadorn, Stephanie Goloway and Susan C., thank you so very much for giving so generously during the campaign.

And thank you, readers of EC and of the other books I've anthologized. I hope you'll enjoy this book too. I think it's a humdinger.

Kate Wolford
Anthologist

Thank you for reading!

We hope you'll leave an honest review at Amazon, Goodreads, or wherever you discuss books online.

Leaving a review helps readers like you discover they books they'll love, and shows support for the authors and editors who worked so hard to create this book.

Please sign up for our newsletter for news about upcoming titles, submission opportunities, special discounts, & more.

WorldWeaverPress.com/newsletter-signup

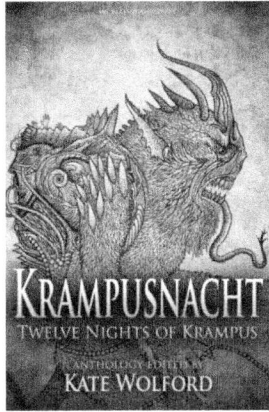

KRAMPUSNACHT: TWELVE NIGHTS OF KRAMPUS
A Christmas Krampus anthology
Edited by Kate Wolford

For bad children, a lump of coal from Santa is positively light punishment when Krampus is ready and waiting to beat them with a stick, wrap them in chains, and drag them down to hell—all with St. Nick's encouragement and approval.

Krampusnacht holds within its pages twelve tales of Krampus triumphant, usurped, befriended, and much more. From evil children (and adults) who get their due, to those who pull one over on the ancient "Christmas Devil." From historic Europe, to the North Pole, to present day American suburbia, these all new stories embark on a revitalization of the Krampus tradition.

Whether you choose to read *Krampusnacht* over twelve dark and scary nights or devour it in one *nacht* of joy and terror, these stories are sure to add chills and magic to any winter's reading.

"From funny to pure terror…This is a must-read for the upcoming holiday season."
— Bitten By Books

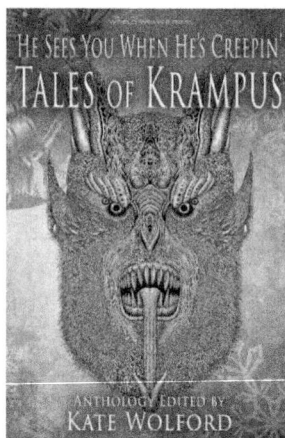

HE SEES YOU WHEN HE'S CREEPIN': TALES OF KRAMPUS
Edited by Kate Wolford

Krampus is the cloven-hoofed, curly-horned, and long-tongued dark companion of St. Nick. Sometimes a hero, sometimes a villain, within these pages, he's always more than just a sidekick. You'll meet manifestations of Santa's dark servant as he goes toe-to-toe with a bratty Cinderella, a guitar-slinging girl hero, a coffee shop-owning hipster, and sometimes even St. Nick himself. Whether you want a dash of horror or a hint of joy and redemption, these 12 new tales of Krampus will help you gear up for the most "wonderful" time of the year.

Featuring original stories by Steven Grimm, Lissa Marie Redmond, Beth Mann, Anya J. Davis, E.J. Hagadorn, S.E. Foley, Brad P. Christy, Ross Baxter, Nancy Brewka-Clark, Tamsin Showbrook, E.M. Eastick, and Jude Tulli.

"These stories were well chosen, and this anthology is perfect for those of you that like Nightmare Before Christmas and other Halloween/Christmas crosses. This one is worth checking out if you like unique and interesting stories."
—Hollie Ohs Book Reviews

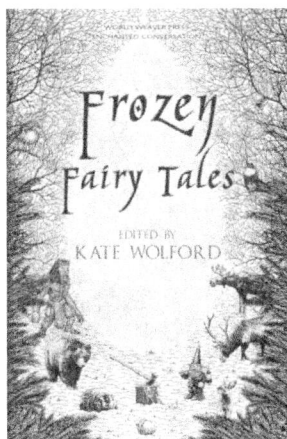

FROZEN FAIRY TALES

Edited By Kate Wolford

Winter is not coming. Winter is here.

As unique and beautifully formed as a snowflake, each of these fifteen stories spins a brand new tale or offers a fresh take on an old favorite like Jack Frost, The Snow Queen, or The Frog King. From a drafty castle to a blustery Japanese village, from a snow-packed road to the cozy hearth of a farmhouse, from an empty coffee house in Buffalo, New York, to a cold night outside a university library, these stories fully explore the perils and possibilities of the snow, wind, ice, and bone-chilling cold that traditional fairy tale characters seldom encounter.

In the bleak midwinter, heed the irresistible call of fairy tales. Just open these pages, snuggle down, and wait for an icy blast of fantasy to carry you away. With all new stories of love, adventure, sorrow, and triumph by Tina Anton, Amanda Bergloff, Gavin Bradley, L.A. Christensen, Steven Grimm, Christina Ruth Johnson, Rowan Lindstrom, Alison McBain, Aimee Ogden, J. Patrick Pazdziora, Lissa Marie Redmond, Anna Salonen, Lissa Sloan, Charity Tahmaseb, and David Turnbull to help you dream through the cold days and nights of this most dreaded season.

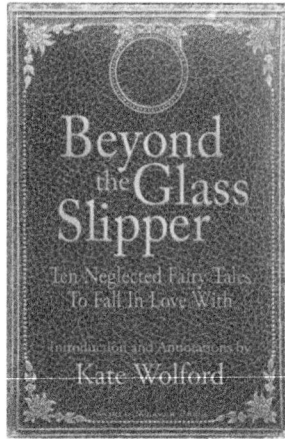

BEYOND THE GLASS SLIPPER

Ten Neglected Fairy Tales to Fall In Love With
With Annotations by Kate Wolford

Some fairy tales everyone knows—these aren't those tales. These are tales of kings who get deposed and pigs who get married. These are ten tales, much neglected. Editor of *Enchanted Conversation: A Fairy Tale Magazine*, Kate Wolford, introduces and annotates each tale in a manner that won't leave novices of fairy tale studies lost in the woods to grandmother's house, yet with a depth of research and a delight in posing intriguing puzzles that will cause folklorists and savvy readers to find this collection a delicious new delicacy.

Beyond the Glass Slipper is about more than just reading fairy tales—it's about connecting to them. It's about thinking of the fairy tale as a precursor to *Saturday Night Live* as much as it is to any princess-movie franchise: the tales within these pages abound with outrageous spectacle and absurdist vignettes, ripe with humor that pokes fun at ourselves and our society.

Never stuffy or pedantic, Kate Wolford proves she's the college professor you always wish you had: smart, nurturing, and plugged into pop culture.

World Weaver Press, LLC
Publishing fantasy, paranormal, and science fiction.
We believe in great storytelling.

WorldWeaverPress.com

Printed in Great Britain
by Amazon